Graphic consequences

By Elaine Jamyson

Printed in the United States of America

First Printing, 2019

ISBN 978-0-9896686-2-0

Cover design and interior artwork by Kobie Livsey.

This is a work of fiction. Names, characters, businesses, places, events and incidents are either the products of the author's imagination or used in a fictitious manner. Apart from Salon Dolce, any resemblance to actual persons, living or dead, or actual events is purely coincidental. The use of Salon Dolce was with the express consent of its owner.

1

Mystery. Intrigue. Deception. Murder amidst comic heroes??? Jess Turner and Lt. Tory Trent again find themselves working together on an extraordinary case. They must use their skills and imaginations to find the real villain in a Hall of Heroes.

ase and Aunt Betty

Prologue

The drive home from the hospital was quiet. Jess was silently crying, mulling over what the doctor had told her. She was going to be a mother!

Jess' best friend, Tami, was driving, respecting the silence. She was worried about how her friend was going to deal with the situation.

Finally, Jess broke the silence that loomed in the car, thick like fog on the ocean. "What am I going to tell my mother? I told her about the gang attack a few months prior, but I could not bring myself to tell her that I had been raped – and by several different men."

Tami had been Jess' friend long enough to know better than to voice her opinion yet. Jess had more to say, and once she was interrupted, she would not continue to speak.

"Then, at my assignment for work, I get kidnapped and conked on the head. I know she is going to think sign language interpreting is a dangerous job and she will want me to stop.

"The attack was around four months ago. That means I am about four months pregnant. What am I supposed to do with a baby?"

"Jess, honey, whatever you decide to do, I am here for you. I am serious. Whether you tell your mother or not,

3

I support your decision. I do suggest, however, that you talk to your Lieutenant."

"Why does everyone call him **_MY_** Lieutenant?"

"Well, _I_ don't have a handsome police officer on _my_ speed dial."

CHAPTER ONE

Lieutenant Tory Trent was pacing in his small, tidy office. He was a large man, well over six feet tall. His pacing basically consisted of taking three steps, turning around, and taking three more steps.

Lt. Trent had just closed an intriguing case at Sebastian Middle School. The case itself was not what was causing him to pace. It was Jess Turner, the sign language interpreter whom he had met on another case who filled his mind. She had unwittingly gotten involved in the middle school case as well as Trent's personal life.

Now, even though he had closed his case, he still felt something was left unresolved. He decided to follow his gut and call Jess.

Jess was still in the car with Tami when the phone rang.

"Well, you talked him up, Tami. The Lieutenant is calling. Should I take the call?"

"Girl, if you don't, I will pull this car over and put you out."

Jess smiled and remembered why she loved her best friend so much. She tried to sound calm when she answered the phone.

"Hello."

5

"Hi Jess. It's Lt. Trent. I called the hospital and they told me you had been released. I hope you are feeling better."

"Yes, I am, and I will take it easy. Tami is driving me home now."

"Good. I will check on you in a couple of days. I just needed to know that you are OK."

As Jess entered her home, she remembered that her mother was out of town visiting her brother and began to panic. "Tami, I don't want to be here alone tonight. Please stay. I know you need to get home to your family. But I need you."

"I am staying. If you think I am just going to drop you off and leave you, you don't know me well at all. I have already called my husband and kids and let them know that it might be a while before I come home.

"But for now, I am going to go walk Petey for you, and then I will make you some lunch."

Petey, Jess' chocolate Labrador, was following the two women through the house, very much aware that something was not right with his owner.

"Don't worry, Petey. I'm OK now."

****

6

Hear Our Hands, a sign language interpreting agency, was founded by Jess and two of her friends, Dylan Shumaker and Sophia Sanchez. As Jess walked through the front door early the next morning, she smiled, proud of what she had accomplished. She still got sad a little as she looked at the plaque dedicated to her deaf twin sister, Jazz, who was killed by a hit and run driver when they were young. Jazz was Jess' inspiration and her memory helped Jess get back to work.

Jess went to the computer and started working on payroll paperwork. She was still diligently working two hours later when Dylan and Sophia came in.

"You are back! Did the doctor say you could return to work?" "How are you? Are you supposed to be back at work?" Dylan and Sophia both talked at the same time. They smothered Jess with hugs and kisses and all she could do was grin.

"I'm fine guys. I feel great and I am happy to be back."

"I still think you should wait before going back in the field." Dylan was very concerned.

"I promise, I am OK. I am not going back to Sebastian Middle School, but I do think I am ready for some other assignments."

"Once your mind is made up, we know you will do what you want. Please be careful." Sophia gave her another hug as she went to begin her work.

Not long after, Sophia frowned. "Jess, are you feeling up to doing a job? We need someone to cover a child support enforcement orientation. It will be a couple of hours long." Sophia didn't want Jess returning to work so soon after leaving the hospital, but she felt this would be safe enough.

"Sure. Give me the address and all of the other information."

CHAPTER TWO

Jess knew that her colleagues had apprehensions about her going back into the interpreting world so soon. She was also aware that they would be even more concerned once she told them she was pregnant. For this

8

reason, she chose not to tell them. They would know soon enough.

Downtown Atlanta was very busy on this autumn day. However, the nip in the air let everyone know that winter was on the way. Jess looked around excitedly as she drew her jacket closer to her. People were rushing around hither and thither, not paying attention to each other. This was Atlanta and Jess loved the feeling it gave her!

She hurried up the steps of the government building even though she was early. She liked to be a few minutes early to her appointments because one never knew what might happen.

This day it paid off. She had to go through a series of security checkpoints before they let her into the elevator that led to her floor. As she rode up in the elevator, she realized the session was due to begin in five minutes.

Leaving the elevator, the receptionist directed her to the third door on the right. There was a large sign that read "Child Support Orientation Meeting" on the door, so Jess knew she was in the right place.

"Write down you first and last name, the name of each child you are trying to collect child support on and the name of the father." The lady at the front of the room rattled off in a bored tone as Jess walked in.

"Good morning. I am Jess Turner. I am a sign language interpreter."

"Sweetie, I don't care what you do for a living. Just sign in."

Jess smiled. "I am not here as a participant. You have a deaf mother in attendance, and she will require my services as an interpreter."

"Oh, OK. Good. That way you can fill out her paperwork and answer her questions. Where is she?"

"Well, her name, according to my records, is Gena Jones and I will only be interpreting today. I will not be filling out her paperwork. If she has any questions, she will ask you, and you can assist her."

"That's silly," the woman rolled her eyes and sighed. "If she is deaf, how is she going to ask me questions?"

"That is where I come in as the interpreter. I will let you know what she says, and I will let her know what you say."

Jess could tell that the woman was not comprehending what she was saying.

"Fine. Which one is she? You can go and sit next to her."

"I don't know. I was hoping you knew who she was. Why don't I check the sign in sheet and see if she has signed in?"

As Jess walked to check the sign in sheet, she knew that this assignment was going to test her patience. On almost every job, an interpreter had to take the time out to educate the parties involved on how to use an interpreter. However, this lady was resistant to the information Jess was trying to share.

She looked over the list and she did not see Gena Jones' name. She went back over to the woman to let her know.

"Well, where is she? She didn't ride with you?"

"No ma'am. I work for an agency and they sent me over. I have never met Ms. Jones in my life, and I do not know where she is. I will sit and wait for a few minutes to see if she shows up."

That seemed to pacify the woman and she went on attending to the others.

At 10 am, the woman closed the doors. "The training will begin now. Please take out your packets and follow along with me. I will explain how to fill out each section."

She walked over to Jess and handed her a packet. "You can start filling out Ms. Jones' packet for her. She is late and I will not review. There are too many people in here."

In reply, Jess said to her: "You can hold the packet for Ms. Jones'. I am not sure she is coming, and I do not want to be responsible for her documents."

The woman rolled her eyes and with an extremely audible sigh, she walked away.

Jess kept watch on the door for Gena Jones. Five minutes into the presentation, a young lady walked in with a baby in a stroller. She looked around and caught Jess' eye. She signed *"Interpreter?"* and Jess immediately indicated that she was.

Jess let Gena know to get a packet from the presenter. Jess stood up and began interpreting for Gena. After a few minutes, the presenter walked over to Jess. "Will you please sit down? Your hand movements are distracting the other participants and they are not paying attention to me."

Jess interpreted what the presenter requested, and Gena informed her that it was OK for Jess to sit down.

"But I do have a question? Gena signed and raised her hand. *Whose birthday do I put on line 17?"* Jess voiced the question. Gena wanted to be sure before she filled in the wrong thing.

The presenter turned around with an exasperated look. "And why do you want to know? You said you were not filling out any paperwork."

Jess took a deep breath. "I apologize for the confusion. Ms. Jones is asking the question."

"Why didn't you say so! You put the birthday of the child on line 17." She turned to Jess. "Why didn't you tell her?"

Jess turned and gave the woman a large smile as she continued interpreting. "Patience is a virtue," she thought.

At the break, Jess introduced herself to Gena.

"Thank you so much for staying. I had a hard time getting through security. I didn't know it would take so long."

"I understand. It must have been even harder with the baby. But no worries, you made it." Jess began to play with the baby.

For the first time, she started to think about how her life was going to change when she had her baby. The feeling was not something she would describe as pleasant. Since the loss of her sister, Jess was used to being a lone wolf. She took care of herself. It was a major change in her life when her mother moved in with her. She loved her mother and had no problem taking care of her while she was battling breast cancer. Yet, at times, she missed her solitude. Once the baby was born, there would not be any more solitude.

"Your baby is beautiful. Is it a girl or a boy?"

"It is a boy. His name is Gordon. He is named after his father. But his dad is no good, so that is why I am here today. Do you have any children?"

The question totally threw Jess off guard. The anxiety began to well up inside of her and she did not know how to answer.

"Ummm, uh, no."

Gena appeared to be baffled by the response. "Why not? You are not getting any younger. Soon you will be too old. You need to have babies now."

Jess took no offense to Gena's reply. She was accustomed to the way of the Deaf community, where individuals were very blunt and spoke their minds freely. There was no malice intended behind Gena's comment and Jess was aware of this.

Jess smiled. "You never know. I might just have several children one day."

Jess was thankful when the facilitator began the class again. She was not prepared to discuss her current situation with family and friends, no less a stranger. But then, her mind began to wander as Gena was filling out her forms. Would Jess have to come here to get child support for her child? Would she have to go with several other young unwed mothers and beg the government for assistance?

This was not the life that Jess wanted to live. But did she have a choice?

CHAPTER THREE

Samuel Guthrie, the head of the notorious gang, the OCs, shook his head in disbelief as he looked at the photographs.

"And where did you say you found these?" He inquired of one of his young commanders.

"I confiscated these pictures from the files that the police have on us."

"But this is not our work. It is a very good forgery, but it is obvious it is not our tag."

"So, what do you want me to do?"

"Stay put where you are and keep me posted on what the police think they have on us. I am going to find out who is copying our graffiti."

As the young man walked away, Guthrie thought about how useful it was to have a man on the inside at the police department.

CHAPTER FOUR

"I'm looking for Lt. Tory Trent!" A hush fell over the usually bustling bullpen as a tall blonde woman with a curvy physique walked through. She walked like she meant business, apparently unaware that men were gawking at her.

"Will someone just direct me to his office?" She impatiently asked.

"No need. Here I am. Why don't you come this way?" Lt. Trent had no idea who this young lady was, but he had an idea that he was in for an adventure.

Trent closed the door of his office. "Please have a seat. Now, how can I assist you?" Trent's dimpled smile was enough to melt anyone's heart.

"Hi. I'm Ginny Colfax. I'm your new partner."

The smile slowly faded from Trent's face. "I beg your pardon, ma'am. I believe there has been some mistake. I don't work with partners."

"Well, you do now. The directive has come down from above. I am your new partner."

Trent stood up slowly. "If you would please excuse me." He swiftly walked out of his office.

Trent rushed outside, deep in thought. How could they do this him? Everyone knew that he did not work with partners. Why are they forcing one on him and now?

The cool, autumn air was a welcome change to the stale air of the bullpen. Outside, he felt he could think clearly about the situation.

Instead of rushing to tell off the powers that be, he decided to ride this wave out. Maybe it was time to turn over a new leaf.

He was still very unhappy about how he was informed of the change. Why didn't anyone warn him?

None of that was important now. He had a partner and he was going to have to deal with it. At least she was easy on the eyes.

Trent was smiling again as he walked back into the bullpen. He noticed that Colfax did not waste any time getting to know those whom she would be working with. Her lighthearted laugh could be heard as the rookies and old-timers told jokes to try to impress her.

Trent walked up to her and extended his hand. "My apologies. Please excuse my rudeness."

Colfax smiled warmly. "Don't worry about it. You were a lot calmer than I expected you to be. I had been briefed about your lack of desire for a partner. I hope I will not be a huge thorn in your side."

"That remains to be seen."

****

When Jess returned to Hear Our Hands, she went into her office and shut the door. It was an unspoken rule that when the door was shut, Jess did not want to be disturbed.

She logged onto her private computer and started looking up adoption agencies. Her time at the child support office today helped her make up her mind that raising a child was not for her. Abortion was not an option. Jess had done some interpreting work for an adoption agency before, so she knew most of what was involved in the process. But, most of all, she wanted the entire affair to go away.

In her studies, Jess found out that there were support groups for victims who have been raped and became pregnant. She seriously considered joining one. Maybe she would even take Tami with her for moral support.

Jess felt more confident as she opened the door to her office and stood face to face with Lt. Tory Trent.

19

"Hi. I was in the area and thought I would stop by."

Jess looked around Trent and noticed a stunning woman with him. Her look narrowed and she mumbled to herself, "I knew you were too good to be true."

Trent seemed unaware that she had spoken. "Let me introduce you to my new partner. This is Detective Ginny Colfax. I wanted you to be one of the first to meet her."

Jess watched as the woman approached with an extended hand. She remembered something about Trent not working with partners. Where did this one come from and why did she have to be so beautiful?

Jess composed herself, extended her hand and smiled.

Trent continued: "I am filling in Colfax on all of my open cases. Since yours is one of them, I thought we could come by for a visit. I also explained to her that you recently helped me solve a case at Sebastian Middle School."

"I was impressed by your bravery, Ms. Turner. I hope you are recuperating nicely."

"Yes, I am. I appreciate your kind words. It is good to know that the police department is still working on figuring out who did this to me.

"Detective Colfax, if you ever need sign language interpreting services, just give us a call."

Ginny Colfax returned the smile. "I surely will. My uncle is deaf, and he lives in the mountains. It is difficult to get interpreters for him. Since I now know an agency, I will give him the number."

"Well, thank you. We will do our best to provide him superior service."

As if on cue, Sophia entered and greeted Colfax. "I will be glad to give you an information packet if you would just follow me."

As Sophia and Colfax went back into the main office, Lt. Trent moved closer to Jess.

"I am glad that you decided to go back to work. I have been concerned about you."

Jess let out a deep breath. "I am not going to lie to you. Things have been hard. But I am trying not to let all these negative events get to me. I have been staying busy."

"Good. Don't let what happened to you keep you from living. You survived because you are a survivor. We need to work together to solve your case, but we need to make some time for play as well."

Jess did not reply. She just looked at Trent with a puzzled expression on her face.

"Jess, a friend of mine has a booth at GraphiCon and I have agreed to man it for a couple of days. It's in a couple of weeks. Will that give you enough time to get ready?"

"GraphiCon!? What is that and what does it have to do with me?"

"I want you to go along with me for at least one day." An amused Trent slyly glanced at Jess to gauge her reaction.

"You still haven't answered my question as to what GraphiCon is."

"Some things are better experienced than explained." At that, Trent turned and walked out of the office, leaving Jess speechless.

****

"Just as you asked, I have found an all-female support group that will allow me to attend with you. They have a meeting tonight at 7 pm. I'm free. Wanna go?"

Jess thought for a moment. She really didn't want to go, yet, she did want to get on the healing path.

"I will go. But if I don't like it, we don't have to go back, right?"

"Deal. I don't want you to do anything you are not ready for."

"No worries. I can do this as long as you are with me."

****

A little house in the middle of an older neighborhood was the location of the support group. Upon entering, it was obvious that the foyer was converted into a reception area. Jess could smell fresh baked cookies. She smiled as she signed in.

"What are you smiling about?"

"I think I smell oatmeal raisin cookies. You know they are my favorite. Maybe it was not such a bad idea to come here."

The room was not set up in a circle, as she thought it would be. It was set up in rows. There were three rows, then another set of three rows perpendicular to the first. The last group of chairs were perpendicular to the ones before. Jess was thankful for this because she was dreading a circle.

"Help yourself, honey. Eat all you want. I think Zelda just took some oatmeal raisin cookies out of the oven. I'm Betty. I don't think I have met you before."

"No, you haven't. This is my first time. My name is Jess, and this is my friend Tami."

"Well, welcome. This is a very comforting group. I hope you find the solace you are looking for."

The girls sat down. They figured the meeting would involve everyone standing up, saying their name and telling their story. It was nothing like that.

Betty commenced right at 7. "Ladies, welcome. I just want to take moment to ensure everyone that this is a safe place. We are all victims or friends of victims. And yes, I said we. I am a victim as well.

"Today we are going to talk about different coping strategies. What are some strategies you have used?"

One lady with a very rosy personality raised her hand. Her makeup was impeccable. Jess couldn't help but think about how beautiful she was.

"I have found that swimming proves to be very therapeutic for me. I have started going to the pool three times a week. If I happen to have a bad day where I can't get a memory out of my head, I add another day."

"On a similar vein, I have been working out. I am trying not to be a fanatic, but I do go every morning before I go to work." This comment was shared by a lady dressed in workout clothes.

A rosy faced, elderly woman remarked: "Making candles has been soothing to me."

A pregnant young lady chimed in. "Puzzles help me to cope. It takes a lot of mental thinking to put a puzzle together. That means I can't think of negative events."

"I love reading. I go into my library, light my fireplace and curl up in my favorite chair." Jess surprised herself.

Betty seemed pleased with everyone's comments. "I hope that these techniques will help all of you."

****

"Correct me if I'm wrong, but I believe that went well." Tami was optimistic about the evening's events.

"I agree. It was nothing like I expected. Still, I don't think I would have survived without my best friend with me."

Tami soaked up the compliments. "Your bestie sounds like an awesome person. You might need to keep her around."

"Whatever! You know I am never letting you go. Besides, if you ever try to leave me, I will stalk you."

The two women giggled like schoolgirls. Jess thought about how refreshing it was to let go.

"Speaking of relaxing," it was if Tami read her mind, "you never told me about GraphiCon. Spill it!"

"Well, a guy was murdered, so . . ."

"Jessica Alison Turner! If you don't start talking about GraphiCon, I will put you out of this car."

"I'm going to stop letting you drive if you keep threatening to put me out of the car."

"Well, I'm really going to do it if you don't start talking about the date you and Tory had."

The word 'date' slapped Jess in her thoughts. Was their trip to GraphiCon really a date?

"Ok. Fine. Let's go grab a bite to eat before we go home, and I will tell you all about it."

CHAPTER FIVE

"Honey!! I think it is time!! Get the car!!!"

Wayne Stern was engrossed in the football game that was on. "What did you say, Sara?" Sara was hard of hearing and at times hard to understand.

Since her husband did not know sign language, she had to yell:

"I SAID THE BABY'S COMING!!!"

Sara read his lips as he said, "OK, OK. The game is almost over. Can you wait five more minutes?"

"Sure thing, Sweetie." The sarcasm dripped from Sara's voice.

She gathered her bag as well as the keys and went to the garage. She made a lot of noise because she wanted

27

Wayne to hear her. She could not believe that he was more interested in that football game than his own child being born.

Sara clutched the car door as a wave of pain took over her body. She yelled out in pain as warm fluid flowed down her legs. As the pain subsided, she did not even bother to change her clothes. She grabbed a towel from the dryer in the garage, laid it out on the driver side seat and sat down. No need to mess up the leather seats. She knew she had about five minutes before the next wave of pain hit.

She put the car in reverse and sped out of the garage.

Wayne cheered as his team made the game winning touchdown.

****

Atlanta General Hospital's maternity area was full of women in various stages of labor. Some women were walking around the hospital floor to help speed up the labor. Others were sitting in the waiting rooms with their family and friends waiting for a bed. Still others were in triage having their vitals and the babies' vitals monitored.

Sara Stern walked into the front desk just as another contraction hit. "My water has already broken, and my contractions are 3 ½ minutes apart.   I need a doctor now!!!"

The receptionist was looking down at her paperwork when she asked, "What is your name and who is your doctor?"

Sara did not understand and explained that she was hard of hearing and needed to read the woman's lips.

The receptionist was very accommodating and asked the question again, this time looking at Sara. She then paged her doctor immediately. She called a nurse to escort Sara to the back, because she could see that her clothes were soiled from the fluids.

"Is Mr. Stern here with you?" She made sure she was facing Sara.

"No, he is not.   The football game was more important this afternoon."

The nurse look at her apologetically. "Well, we will make sure that we take extra special care of you. Would you like an interpreter?"

Sara shook her head "No".

"OK. Let's start by getting you in a dry gown. Then we will hook you up to the monitor to make sure the baby is OK."

Sara changed her clothes, laid on the hospital bed and allowed the process to begin. This was her and her husband's first child and she wanted to make sure that everything went OK. However, she did not feel OK. She believed that something was not right.

Later, the doctor arrived and gently held her hand. "Sara, you are doing great. We are a little concerned about the baby's heart rate though. We might have to do a c-section. Remember that we discussed that this might be a possibility?"

"Yes. That is fine. As long as my baby is OK."

"OK. We will prep you for the surgery. Is your husband here? He will be able to be in the room with you the entire time."

"He is not here now. We do not need to wait for him, though, if the baby is in distress. I will be fine."

CHAPTER SIX

Colfax was not going to let the visit to Jess Turner's office go by without question. "So, how long have the two of you been dating?"

"We are not dating."

"OK. So how long have the two of you been going out?"

Trent pulled over his car and parked on the side of the road. "I don't like to discuss my private life. I like keeping to myself. You are going to have to forgive me because I am still trying to get used to the idea of even having a partner.

"So, I might not know how to say this in the nicest way, but my personal life is off limits."

"Understood. I have no problem respecting your privacy. I know that having a partner must be difficult for you."

"Thank you. And again, I meant no disrespect."

"None taken."

As Trent drove off, he figured that having a partner might not be as bad as he thought.

****

"I have two questions," Tami liked to get right to the point. "When are you going to tell Trent you are pregnant and what are you wearing to the comic book convention?"

"Tami, I haven't even decided if I am going to go at all."

"I think your lieutenant has made that decision for you. He really didn't give you an option."

"He is right. I do need to enjoy myself a little. I would never have dreamed of going to anything like GraphiCon."

Jess had gone online immediately after Lt. Trent left her office to research GraphiCon. She was not a comic

32

geek or a "fanboy" but could hold her own where there was a debate about who was the greatest superhero of all time.

"I don't care if the man wants to take you to the city dump, you are going. Now, about your pregnancy ..."

"I DON'T KNOW. STOP PRESSURING ME!"

"Look, this is what friends are for, to do the dirty work. This baby is not going to go away just because you don't want to talk about it."

"I know. I'm sorry I yelled at you. I am having a hard time dealing with all of this. I promise I will tell Tory and my mom soon."

****

After watching the game, Wayne Stern decided to do the right thing and check on his unborn child. It was a hard decision because another football game was coming on.

The phone was answered on the first ring. "Hello darling. I am calling to check on you and the baby. Is everything OK?"

"It would be better if you were here with me. When are you going to get here? My contractions are very close together."

33

"I will be there as soon as I can. I am trying my best. I might have a couple of other things to do, but I will be there soon. What hospital is it again?"

The phone line went dead.

CHAPTER SEVEN

Jess woke up sweating and nauseous. She ran to the bathroom and promptly threw up. After washing her face in cold water, she dried her face and looked in the mirror. The reflection that looked back at her seemed a little fuller in the face than she remembered. Jess decided that it was time for her to accept the fact that she was going to have a baby. That was going to mean that she get a few things done in preparation for this event.

She called Sophia and informed her that she would be taking the next couple of days off.

"Are you feeling OK, Jess? Maybe you came back to work too soon. I knew I shouldn't have sent you to work the other day."

"I'm fine, Sophia. I just have some personal business to take care of. No worries. You can call me if you need me for anything."

Jess went into the kitchen and was surprised to see her mother.

Louisa Turner's breast cancer was in remission. She had moved in with Jess during the ordeal. However, she was determined to live her life to the fullest.

That's why it was surprising to Jess to see her mother back early from her latest adventure.

"Mom. You're home!"

"Is that so surprising? I do live here for the moment," her mother snapped.

"I know, but you weren't due back for a couple more days."

"Isn't a lady entitled to change her mind sometimes? I was ready to come home and rest a little."

Immediately, Jess became alarmed. "Mom, how are you feeling? Do I need to call the doctor?"

"Not for me, honey, not for me." Louisa's tone was one that struck terror in Jess' heart. Her mother knew something, and she wasn't happy about it.

"What is it, Mom?"

"I thought I raised you right. I tried to shelter you and your sister, Jazz, and I failed miserably when it came to her. Now you. You have been attacked twice in less than a year and you refuse to talk to me about it. So, I gave you your space.

"Now you are hiding something from me, and I wish you could talk to me. I am your mother!"

Jess sighed. She hated when her mother blamed herself for Jazz's death. She also knew there was no way to comfort her mother when she was in this mood. She remained silent.

Louisa continued. "Then, I hear from Shirley Askew that her daughter saw you at a child support enforcement meeting downtown, filling out paperwork. When were you going to tell me you are pregnant?"

"Mom, it's complicated . . ."

"No, it isn't. All you had to do was say, 'Mom, I got knocked up.' I shouldn't have to receive a text message from someone I don't really like with that information.

"You are my daughter. Why couldn't you just tell me? I hear you throwing up in the mornings. I see that your face is getting puffy. Didn't you know I would figure it out?" At this point, Louisa was shouting.

Jess calmly walked to the table and sat down. "Mom, please come and have a seat. I have something to tell you."

"No need to tell me. I already know. I just can't believe you would go off and get pregnant without being married. I raised you better than that.

"You know how much you work. Who is supposed to watch the baby when you are not here? Me? NO SIR!!!"

"Mom, please sit down. We need to talk."

"I have other things to do."

"Mother, for the love of Jazz, please sit down!"

Mentioning Jazz was not something Jess wanted to do, but she knew she would get her mother's attention.

Louisa sat down at the table. Jess got up and moved her chair so that she was sitting at her mother's side.

After taking hold of her mother's hand, Jess began. "Mom, when I was attacked a few months ago, I was raped. It was a gang initiation, so I was violated by several men.

"It wasn't until after the events at Sebastian Middle School that I found out I am pregnant.

"I didn't want to tell you everything because you are going through so much and do not need the added stress. I was not sure when to tell you, I don't even know what to do with the baby. I am very confused right now."

Louisa looked at her daughter, hugged her to her and began sobbing.

"I didn't protect you either. Honey, I am so sorry. I said some hurtful things to you. Please forgive me."

"No need for forgiveness, Mom. It's OK. Communication is not one of our strong points."

Ironically, between the two women, they could speak or sign seven languages.

"Sweetheart, do you want to talk about what happened to you? I will clear my schedule for the morning."

"I really don't feel like rehashing events that I have spent months trying to forget."

"Honey, what do you want me to do to help you?"

"First of all, tell Shirley Askew and her daughter to mind their own business. After that, I'm really not sure."

****

Wayne Stern knew that he was in big trouble. He was not present during the birth of his child, and even he knew this was a huge mistake. As he drove to the hospital, he decided to stop at a flower shop. Maybe he could redeem himself with roses.

He walked into the store, smiling to himself about how brilliant he was.

"May I have a bouquet of 2 dozen roses with all the extras?" He knew one dozen was not enough. "I am taking these to the maternity section of the hospital."

"Sir, hospitals do not allow flowers on the maternity floors. But we do have some balloon arrangements." The boredom in the young man's voice was hard to miss.

"OK Fine."

"What size vase would you like, sir?" The clerk didn't even bother to look up from his computer.

"It doesn't matter. You decide. I will take two arrangements with all the fixings."

The disinterested clerk selected the most expensive vases with the most elaborate arrangements he could find.

"How would you like to pay for this?"

Forty-five minutes later, Wayne was whistling as he carefully made his way to the car. He opened the back door and gingerly placed them in. He even took the time out to buckle the balloons in carefully so as not to crush them.

****

Sara Stern was still groggy from the medication given to her during her c-section. They had brought the baby to her briefly. She had a beautiful baby girl. She couldn't hear what the nurses were saying. Something was wrong and the nurses whisked her baby away to NICU.

As much as she tried to fight it, Sara drifted off to sleep.

CHAPTER EIGHT

Jess still was not feeling well and the conversation with her mom did not make her feel any better.

She went into her home library and flopped into her favorite chair. She pulled out her tablet from the side pocket of her recliner and began looking for OBGYNs who accepted her insurance.

She found a few and called to get an appointment at Dr. Johnson' office. They had an opening at 2 pm. She decided to take the appointment.

Jess suddenly felt depressed after hanging up the phone with the doctor's office. She knew it was foolish, but it felt like she was making a commitment by going to the doctor.

She started crying, deep, throaty sobs. The more she cried, the worse she felt, yet she couldn't stop weeping. Her mother came into her library and held her.

That simple gesture made Jess stop crying. Her mother was not a "hugger" and she hadn't really been in her mother's arms this many times since Jazz's death.

"Mom, I know you don't like doctors, but how do you feel about coming with me to my first prenatal appointment. I do not want to go alone."

"Yes, baby. I will be there with you."

****

The officer was able to exit the evidence room undetected. He replaced the artwork that supposedly belonged to the OCs and went on about his business. No one even suspected that there was a mole in the department. Or so he thought.

****

Jess and Louisa walked into the doctor's office and were transported to a different world. The tranquil sounds of ocean waves were being piped through strategically placed speakers. The aroma that flooded the room was that of crisp, clean air. The pictures on the wall were of beautiful beach scenes.

For a moment, Jess forgot her reason for coming. Next to being in the mountains at her grandfather's cabin, the beach was her favorite place to be. It wasn't until her mother nudged her towards the front desk that reality came crashing back.

The receptionist was pleasant and asked Jess for the necessary information. Next, Jess took the time to meticulously fill out the several packets of paperwork the office needed from her.

"There is more paperwork here than when I bought my house. I feel like they want my entire life story."

"Make sure you don't forget anything, Jess. They need to know breast cancer runs in your family." Louisa was not sure what role Jess wanted her to play, but she decided that she would just be mom.

Jess sensed her mother's apprehensions. She leaned over and gave her a big hug. "Thanks for being here with me. I really need you."

After about twenty minutes, the nurse called Jess back. "Come on, Mom. I can't do this alone."

Jess and Louisa were shown to a room after Jess was weighed and her blood pressure was taken.

"You know the drill, honey. Take everything off, except your undies and put on the gown. It needs to open in the front." The nurse was very friendly, and Jess even allowed herself to relax a little while they waited on the doctor.

The doctor came in wearing a T-shirt that read "Life's a beach" underneath his lab coat. He had on jeans and tennis shoes and Jess began to wonder if she had chosen the right office.

"Well, hello Ms. Turner. How are you feeling today? And since I see the family resemblance, I am going to assume you are Ms. Turner's sister. Am I right?"

Before Jess could answer, Louisa chimed in.

"Doctor, you are too kind. But this is my daughter."

"That is unbelievable. You must have had her when you were still in diapers." Dr. Johnson was racking up all kinds of points with Louisa.

Louisa giggled and began to blush.

"Well, my lady, we are going to check out your new grandchild today." He turned towards Jess. "Are you ready, Ms. Turner?"

"As ready as I will ever be. And please, call me Jess."

"And you can call me Louisa."

Jess rolled her eyes at her mother as the doctor performed a quick exam.

"OK, here is the part we have all been waiting for. You are far enough along. Ready to see the baby?"

Dr. Johnson seemed more excited than the two women as he called in the ultrasound technician.

Jess and Louisa strained to make out the body parts of the baby on the screen. It had a strong heartbeat and was constantly moving.

"It is going to be difficult to determine gender today. I cannot get a clear shot. The baby seems a little excited today." The ultrasound technician continued to press on Jess' abdomen, trying to get a better angle. "How far along are you? The baby seems big. Are you sure of when you got pregnant?"

"Very." Jess lay on the table, trying to feel some sort of connection to the baby. Yet, she didn't seem to be able to feel any attachment to it.

Dr. Johnson must have sensed this. "Jess, why don't you get dressed and meet me in my office. Louisa, please stay here with Anna and see if she can't print you off some pictures of your new grandchild."

Jess prepared herself for what the doctor might have to tell her. She walked in and the doctor gestured for her to sit down.

"Ms. Turner, Jess, I want you to feel comfortable. I can tell that you are having some difficulty emotionally connecting with your baby."

"Doctor, you are right. I am not even sure that I want to keep it. I guess I am going to distance myself from it."

"I figured something like was happening to you. However, we are past the time where we can terminate the pregnancy. Are you considering giving your baby up for adoption?"

"Stop calling it my baby!" Jess even surprised herself with her outburst.

"Doctor, I am so sorry. I didn't mean to yell at you. I am so confused right now. I don't know what to do."

"Jess, have you considered therapy? It might help for you to have someone to talk to about your situation."

"Maybe I will. I was considering going to some support groups for rape victims. Should I start off by going to a therapist first?"

"The decision is yours to make."

"Dr. Johnson, whatever I decide to do with this baby, I want it to be healthy. What do I need?"

****

"We have to get the baby's room ready. Too bad it moved so much we can't tell if it is a girl or a boy." Louisa talked nonstop on the way home.

"This is so exciting. We are going to have a baby around the house. It has been years. Did you see the sonogram pictures? The baby has your head."

"Mother! I haven't decided that I am going to keep the baby. I am thinking of putting it up for adoption."

"Oh."

47

"Just please give me some time to make my own decision."

"Honey, you have been through a very stressful ordeal. I will give you as much time as you need. Don't pay any attention to my babbling."

"Thanks mom. Another thing, please don't tell anyone. I want to come to terms with my pregnancy before others get involved."

****

Sophia and Dylan sat in the Hear Our Hands office eating their lunch, discussing Jess.

"She has been acting different lately. I blame myself for sending her out on assignment too soon."

Dylan reassured Sophia. "You did not make Jess do anything that she didn't want to do."

Sophia and Dylan knew Jess better than most people. After having met at an interpreter conference, the three of them became inseparable. They helped Jess build her dream of owning her own sign language interpreting agency.

They had become a family when each donated their blood, sweat and tears to the success of Hear Our Hands. When one member was suffering, they all felt it.

"I am not sure that what Jess is going through has anything to do with work. She really hasn't been the same since she was attacked." Dylan reflected thoughtfully as he sipped on his soda.

Sophia sighed. "All I know is that she is not happy. Even that fine policeman doesn't make her genuinely smile. If Detective Dreamy can't make you smile, something is wrong. What are we going to do?"

"Let's give her time. Jess is a private person. She will eventually tell us what she needs.

CHAPTER NINE

Something wasn't right. Not only was Jess acting strange the last time they spoke, she didn't even appear jealous that he had a hot new partner.

Trent reprimanded himself for the thought. He wasn't sure if it was because he called Colfax hot or because Jess wasn't jealous. It wasn't as if they were a couple … yet. Either way, Jess had been through some very trying times recently.

The thought of being in a relationship with Jess made Trent smile and his caramel colored dimples were deeper than ever. He was so deep in thought that he did not see the visitor in the doorway.

"What has you so amused?" Jess loved the sight of Trent's dimples. "Am I interrupting something?"

"No, not at all. Please come in. I was just thinking about giving you a call."

"Really? Am I in trouble?" Jess couldn't' help teasing him.

"Well, that depends. You have not seemed to bounce back from this last episode. Is there anything I can do?" All the humor was gone from Trent's voice.

Jess should have known that a lieutenant as good as Trent would know that something was wrong. She had debated whether to tell him about her pregnancy or not. After discussing it with her mother, she decided that it was best to tell him.

"And not on the phone," Louisa had shouted as she left the house to go shopping with her friends.

The idea seemed good at the time, but now, standing in front of him, Jess almost lost her nerve.

"Lt. Trent. . ."

"Tory."

"Tory, I need to talk to you about something important."

"Hey Trent!! You in there?" Colfax stuck her head into Trent's office. "We have a case and … OH! You have company."

"I was just leaving," Jess assured her. "Thank you for your time LT."

And before Trent could say a word, Jess was gone.

****

"You seemed distracted. Is everything OK?" Colfax questioned her partner.

"Yeah, I'm good." Trent still seemed to be in a fog.

"I know you are a private person. But I am here if you want to talk."

Trent grunted and kept driving. He was not about to discuss his feelings for Jess with Colfax.

51

"Okay. Your loss. But I believe it has something to do with a certain Ms. Turner. I know I interrupted something in your office." Colfax was persistent.

"For someone who is a detective, you are not that observant, are you? I don't want to talk about it!"

"OK, lover boy, OK. I get it."

The next few moments of the ride proceeded in silence. Finally, Trent spoke.

"Colfax, we have had this discussion before. I mean no disrespect, but I like to keep my personal life, well, personal."

"I know. But I need a partner who is focused. And right now, you are not focused."

Trent thought a bit about what she said.

"Agreed. I will put this aside and focus on the task at hand." However, those were just words because Trent could not get Jess off his mind.

****

"Having a baby can't be that difficult. Why do I need to be at the hospital? Isn't that what doctors are for?" Wayne Stern thought as he tried to find a spot in the parking deck. He hated hospitals and he hated missing football. It didn't matter that he recorded all the games and continually watched them over and over. Football was Life. Maybe they will have the football game on in the hospital.

Wayne Stern juggled the balloon bouquets all the way to the reception desk in the hospital.

"Will you please have these delivered? The card in the vase has all of the information."

"Sure sir, but don't you want to take them yourself?"

"Nope. You can do it."

****

Jess took an assignment that she knew would be difficult for her to do but would give her an opportunity to reflect on what she needed to do with her life.

A deaf woman had just given birth at the hospital and she was requesting around the clock interpreting services. Jess decided she would relieve the current interpreter and work from 5 pm to 10 pm.

Deborah, an interpreter who works for Jess' agency was excited to see her.

"Jess, it has been a long time since I've seen you. How are you? I heard about what happened. Such a shame. Are you OK?"

"I am fine, Debbie. I get better each day. How are things here with the patient?" Jess was not really in the mood to talk and not about herself.

"Well, the mother had a c-section because the baby had the umbilical cord wrapped around his neck. He is still in the Newborn Intensive Care Unit. Mom is in a lot of pain."

"OK. Anything else I need to know?"

"The nurse in charge is Annie. She is very nice and will work with you.

"The tech, Laurie, will try to sneak in the room without you because she believes she knows enough sign language to communicate."

"OK. Sounds like fun."

While they were debriefing, Jess saw a woman with a machine for taking vital signs go into the patient's room. Her name tag read "Laurie".

"I see what you mean. Let me go in now. It was good seeing you again, Debbie."

When Jess walked into the room, the tech was wrapping the patient's arm with a blood pressure cuff. Jess took this opportunity to introduce herself to both women.

"Hello. I am Jess. I am the interpreter until 10 pm tonight. Congrats on your baby boy!"

"Hi. I'm Tonya. Thank you. This is my first baby and I had to have a c-section. I am in so much pain."

"I'm Laurie. L-A-U-R-I-E."

Jess interpreted as Laurie continued to wave her hands and clap her hands. "I am fluent in my sign language alphabet."

CHAPTER TEN

GraphiCon! It was not at all what Jess imagined. There were literally people – or should she say characters – everywhere. The attire varied from basic masks and face paints to elaborate costumes complete with electronic weaponry. Aliens beeped, monsters roared, superheroes chased, and villains evaded capture.

Jess was so enthralled in all the colors and sounds that she did not notice Trent walk up beside her. He was visibly amused by her fascination.

"A beautiful young woman should not walk around this crowd unescorted. Please allow me to be your guide." Trent's dimples popped as he did not even try to hide his amusement.

"I had no idea . . ." Jess could not even finish her statement.

Trent looked amazing in his outfit. He had on a T-shirt which showed off his well-toned chest and read 'GraphiCon or bust'. It was black and blended well with his black jeans and black boots.

Trent had no idea that he was the one who took Jess' breath away. "Come on, Jess. We need to get to my table. I will show you things as we walk."

"So why didn't you dress up, Tory? I was half expecting you to show up as a superhero."

"No, that is not my style. I am more of an observer. I enjoy all that is happening around me.

"My friend sells T-shirts. I am sporting one of his designs."

"Well, I like it. I would never have guessed that GraphiCon would be this exciting!"

They chatted as they walked. Finally, they arrived at the booth Trent had to man for the day. It was on the second floor of the building and overlooked the first floor. So, while stationed at their booths, vendors could also see everything happening on the floor below.

Tory schooled Jess on the prices of everything and showed her how to use the tablet to take credit card orders. Jess was having a blast. She took pictures with the interesting characters who stopped at the table. She loved helping customers pick out the right shirt for them. Hours later, she realized that she hadn't enjoyed herself this much in a very long time.

"Jess, are you hungry? I can go and grab us some lunch if you don't mind handling the customers."

"Food would be awesome! I would love a giant, greasy cheeseburger and some fries. I won't even feel guilty about eating it."

"Great. I will go now. If you need anything, just call me."

Time flew as Jess chatted up the customers and watched the shenanigans of the geeked up crowd. When Trent returned with her food, she hadn't even realized how much time had passed.

"This is spectacular! Why didn't I know about this before? It is so unbelievably fun!"

As Jess took a break and ate her lunch, a loud commotion started brewing on the first floor near the windows. People were shouting that a car was swerving out of control outside. As more and more people rushed to look at the car, it became evident that it was going to smash into a nearby pole attached to the building.

As the car crashed into the pole, the noise was deafening. Everything seemed to move in slow motion. The glass on the convention center window exploded as the car came to a halt. It appeared that the pole had almost cut the car in two. Smoke was billowing out of the car as the door on the driver's side was thrown open. Those who were not hurt had gathered inside and outside of the window and people were screaming.

A man covered in blood, began walking like a zombie towards the crowd gathered inside the building. As he took each deliberate step with his hands stretched out in front of him, the crowd began to realize that the entire "accident" was part of his entrance.

"Hey man, your costume is awesome!"

"Dude, you had us fooled smashing your car up like that. Are you a stunt driver?"

The man did not reply. He just kept walking. He spotted a woman with a baby stroller. After glancing at the baby, he grabbed hold of the mother's hand. In a raspy voice, he spit blood as he said, "I have to ..." The mother screamed as he collapsed on a nearby table and became entangled in the tablecloth as he fell to the floor.

Jess saw another man, presumably a doctor, check the man's pulse, and shake his head, letting the others know that the victim was dead.

The crowd became a mob as creatures of all species started screaming and scrambling away from the scene.

"Jess. Stay here. Do not leave this area unless I tell you to. Please tell me that you will stay. I need to know you are safe."

"I promise to stay here. Be careful."

Trent ran off, flashing his badge which was hidden somewhere on him.

Everything after that was a blur to Jess. Time passed. A tow truck was attached to the vehicle, pulling it from the pole. However, it did not remove the vehicle from the scene. The smoke from the car continued to permeate the air.

Despite warnings from officials, the crowd around the accident area grew. Aliens in all colors, shapes and sizes blended with the various superheroes and villains. Jess had a bird's eye view of the whole scene, yet she began to feel as if she was suffocating.

Just at that moment, Trent walked up behind her. "Jess, are you OK? Look at me."

"Tory, I need fresh air. I don't feel so good."

"Let me get you out of here. My friend is here to relieve me at the table. I will introduce you later."

Trent grabbed Jess by the elbow and led her through the masses to the nearest exit. He watched with concern as she took deep breaths in order to regain her composure.

"Thank you. I am much better now. I guess it was too much excitement for me."

"I see. Maybe you are too tired and excited to help me with this new case that just fell into my lap."

"Wait . . . I mean . . . I'm OK now. Are you handling the accident? You mean, it wasn't just an accident?"

"Slow down, Missy. I don't want you to get too excited. Yes, I am handling the accident and no, it was not an accident."

"Wow. I would love to help you. I need a diversion in my life right now. Where do we start?"

CHAPTER ELEVEN

"First things first. I need to hire you."

"Huh?"

"Well, there are some Deaf convention attendees here. They witnessed the accident and we need to interview them. Their interpreter was one of the people injured in the stampede. Can I hire you to take their statements?"

"You don't have to hire me. I can do it for free."

"No, I want to do everything by the book so no one can come back later and say that the investigation was tainted. My department has a fund for this."

"OK. Call my office and make a formal request."

****

Sean Rivers was dressed in a bright yellow bodysuit that left nothing to the imagination. His bright white face mask contrasted with the black eyeholes. As Jess approached and identified herself as the interpreter, Sean removed his mask. His face was flustered, and Jess could tell he was very agitated.

"Finally, an interpreter. I have been waiting."

Jess could tell that he was not happy. She skipped the introductions and nodded for Trent to begin his questions.

"Mr. Rivers, please tell me what happened?"

"My friend and I were looking out of the window and we saw the blue car going very fast in the parking lot. We saw the car crash into the pole. I turned to the side to ask our interpreter if this was part of the show. This is my first time at GraphiCon."

"Was the interpreter facing the window?"

"Yes, everyone was. When I tapped him, he turned around. Then people started running and pushing. The interpreter fell and some people tripped over him.

"I tried to help him, but the crowd pushed me back. I am sorry that he got hurt."

"It is not your fault, Mr. Rivers," Trent assured him. "Did you see anything else that might help us with this case?"

"No. I could not see the driver's face. I just saw the car going fast and get close to the building, and I saw it crash into the pole. I saw the man, but I could not hear if he said anything. You know, I'm deaf."

"Thank you for your statement, Mr. Rivers. If you remember anything else later, here is my card. You can give m a call."

Jess and Trent next interviewed Sean Rivers' friend, who basically had the same story.

"Well, Jess. This is not how I expected your first time at GraphiCon to end up," Trent stated apologetically after the interviews were over. "But you can't say that it was boring."

"The word boring never even crossed my mind. It has been so exciting that my head is spinning."

63

"Well, the fun is not over yet."

"Well, what's next?"

"I don't want you to leave by yourself to go home. We can ride the train together. But I can't leave before I examine the car. Do you want to tag along?"

"You know it!"

****

The front end of the blue car was smashed and ripped open as if a giant had crushed it in his hands. The rear door was open and twisted like a key in a keyhole. Even though the accident had happened a couple of hours earlier, the vehicle was still smoking.

"You need to examine the car. Is that why the truck didn't take it away?"

"Yes."

Trent motioned for Jess to stay back while he inspected the car. He didn't want her to inhale any of the fumes.

"Just what I thought," Trent yelled from the floorboard of the blue wreck. "The brake line has been cut. He would have been able to drive only a few miles before he lost control."

"So, if we find out what's a few miles from here, we can find out where his brakes were cut." Jess was proud of herself for this revelation.

"Looks like you have a junior detective on your hands, Trent," Colfax grinned as she walked up. "No wonder you don't want a partner. Am I interrupting?"

Jess began to blush. "Hello, Detective, . . . um, Colfax, right? Nice to see you again. Trent, I am going to go find a restroom. I will be right back."

Jess fled the scene of the crash. She didn't understand why she got so flustered around Colfax. Or maybe she did understand. She viewed Colfax as competition and Colfax was perfect and smart. Jess was pregnant and . . . pregnant. Ugh!

In the restroom, everyone was talking about the crash.

"Did you see the dead man?" a woman with purple snakes in her hair inquired.

A woman with blood oozing from her head responded. "Yes. He looked like the walking dead. I thought the whole thing was staged at first."

"Nope. He wasn't faking. He was really bleeding and really dead."

Jess came out of the stall and began washing her hands.

"Hey, aren't you working with the police? I saw you over there, checking out the crash with that FINE policeman. So, what do you think happened?" The snake haired woman was now in Jess' face.

Jess backed up a step. "I am just a civilian observer, just like everyone else. I don't know what happened anymore than you do."

"She's lying!" yelled the bloody woman.

"Well, who cares? If she doesn't want to tell us what happened, we will find out on our own."

The two "ladies" left the restroom and slammed the door behind them.

"Well," Jess thought, "not everyone at GraphiCon is pleasant."

Just took a few moments to compose herself. She was almost finished collecting herself and about to leave the restroom when Colfax walked in.

"Hi honey. Just coming to check on you. We are finished up here and Trent was getting worried about you." Colfax laughed. "I told him you are a grown woman and you can take care of yourself."

"I was just on my way out." Jess didn't know what else to say to Colfax. She could tell the other woman was fishing for information that she was not ready to give.

****

"We are missing something. I can just feel it." Trent was pacing in his office.

Colfax was standing in the doorway. "OK. Let's take it from the top. Car gets brakes cut. Car crashes into pole. Driver staggers out and dies. What are you missing?"

"The why. Why were his brakes cut? Why didn't he get out of the car telling us who cut his brakes? Why did he say he had to do something? There are a lot of questions to be answered."

"So, what do you want to do?"

"Let's go check out the car again." Trent grabbed one of his 8 oz Cokes and left his office.

Colfax and Trent arrived at the garage where the car had been towed. It had been split in half to the back seat.

"I looked all through the car as much as I could. It was very hot and smoky at the time. I am going to give it another look over now that it has cooled off."

"And a certain Jess Turner isn't here to distract you."

"Here you go again. Do you just enjoy taunting me?"

"Maybe. Why do you get so flustered when I mention her name?"

"Maybe I should just ask you why you keep mentioning her name to get me flustered. Or are you just mad that I am not swooning over you and falling at your feet.

"Yes, I have done my homework on my new 'partner'. Putting you with me is basically punishment because you keep putting your other partners in compromising situations.

"Well, look here, lady. I am not the one to mess with. If you want to work, fine. If not, move out of my way."

Colfax stood there speechless. Then, she moved towards the car and started picking through the rubbish.

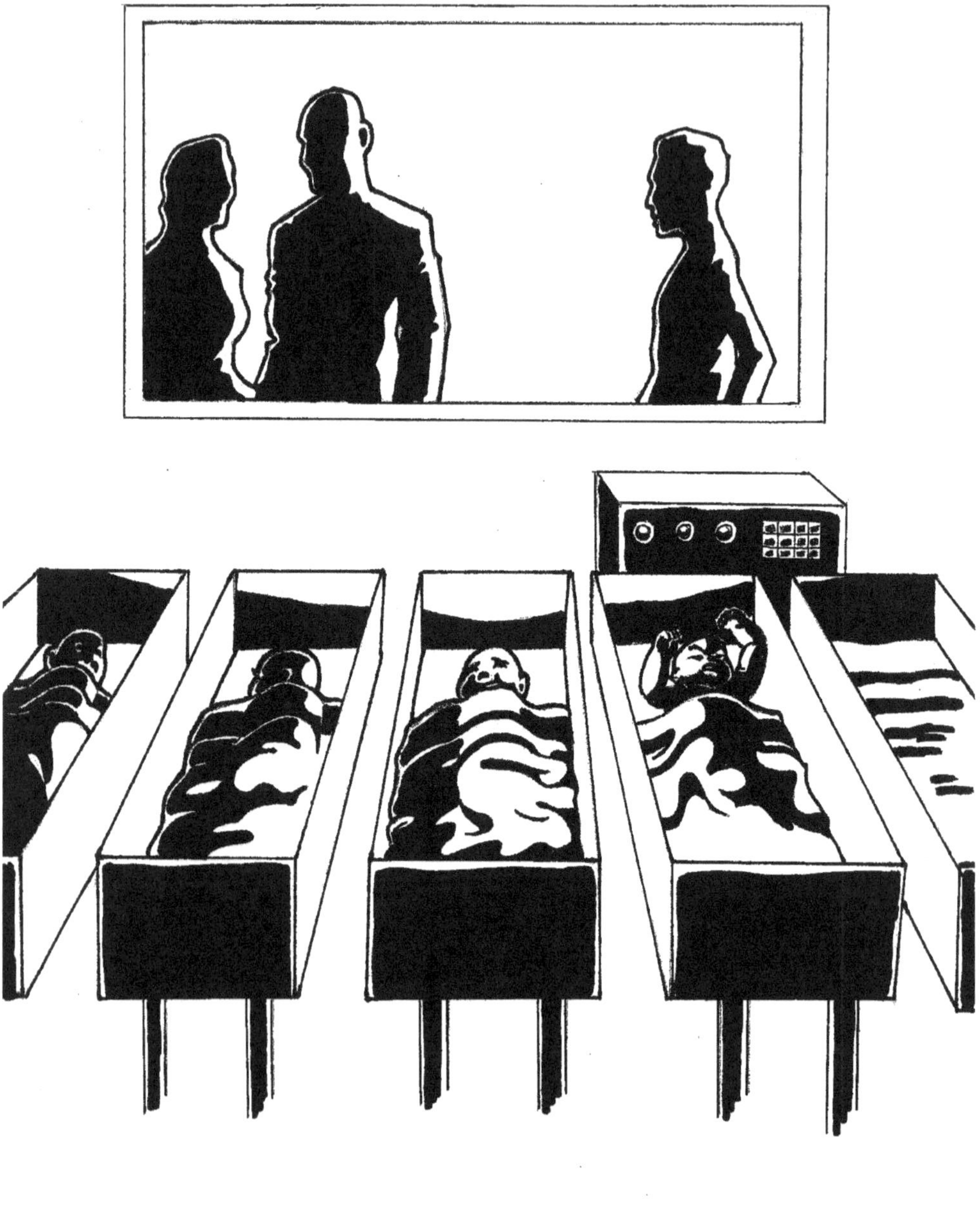

****

The shift at Atlanta General seemed boring compared to all the excitement at GraphiCon. Jess could barely keep her mind on the job at hand. She chose to work the overnight shift. Tonya was sleep most of the night and the nurses didn't bother her.

Jess went to the nursery to look at the babies. That was her favorite part of working on the maternity floor. She was always mesmerized by the miracle of life and looking at the babies always brought her a sense of calm.

The next morning, before her shift was over, Tonya was alert and ready to talk.

"Did you hear that the husband of a hard of hearing woman here in the hospital was killed yesterday. His brakes were cut in his car. It's awful."

"Really?" Jess acted surprised. "How sad."

"Yes, and he and his wife just had a little girl."

She knew she should not get involved, but Jess was curious. She decided to visit the nursery. Watching the babies while they slept was one of Jess' favorite things. She liked to observe the interactions of the nurses with the young infants.

70

While she was looking through the window of the nursery, a woman rolled up in a wheelchair. She lovingly looked at one child.

Jess noticed the hearing aid in the woman's ear. What are the odds that this was the woman whose husband was killed?

Jess faced the window and asked the lady which child belonged to her. The mother didn't respond. It had to be her.

Jess faced the woman. "Hi. How are you?"

"I am a little sore, but that pales in comparison to the joy I feel when I see my baby girl."

"Which baby is yours?"

"You sign! Do you have any deaf family members?"

"I had a deaf twin sister. She died a few years ago."

"Oh, sorry. The second little girl from the left is mine. Her name is Wynter. Oh, and my name is Sara."

"My name is Jess. Your daughter has a beautiful name. Did you pick it out or did her father?

71

Jess knew she was on thin ice, but she had to know. Sara waited a moment before she answered.

"My husband was killed yesterday. I will be raising Wynter on my own."

"I am so sorry! Please accept my condolences. You said killed?"

"Yes, he had a car accident."

CHAPTER TWELVE

Jess was exhausted on the drive home, as she always was when she worked the overnight shift. Yet, she debated as to whether to call Trent or not. Finally, she decided to call.

"Tory. I don't know if this is nothing or if it is major. Can we meet?"

"Sure. I will meet you at the diner in 20 mins."

Jess arrived first. She picked "their" table and waited for him to arrive. She was so engrossed in her self-pity about being pregnant that she did not notice him come in.

"Never sit alone with your back to the door. You never know who might walk up on you." Colfax had no problem teasing Jess. "I see you were not expecting me. I will just pull up another chair.

"No need. Sit down, Colfax and cut it out. I will get another chair." Trent looked at Colfax with a scowl.

"OK. Jess, what do you have?"

73

"Well, I was working the overnight shift at Atlanta General Hospital. I was on the maternity floor. Word is going around the floor that one of the mothers on the floor lost her husband."

"OK. So, what?" Colfax was just a little bitter.

"She said she got a message on her video answering machine that his brakes were cut. She had just had a little girl. And Atlanta General is within the distance of the accident."

"Well Jr. detective, we have already talked to the wife on the maternity floor. You got it wrong. She had a little boy. We found a parking ticket in his car."

"Impossible, I talked to her myself. She said she had a daughter named Wynter."

"Jess." Trent only had to say her name.

"Why would she even talk to you?" Colfax asked with a sneer.

"She saw me signing and just opened up.

"I know I shouldn't have interviewed her. But I was right there when she came to see her baby. She was so distraught. I had to talk to her. And she had a girl! I saw her myself."

"Sara Stern. That's not the person we interviewed. We have a Tamica Parsons. She said she kept her maiden name when they got married. There is no doubt they had a baby boy. They were taking him away to get circumcised while we were there. Her story was corroborated by her brother who was with her.

"She also had a beautiful balloon bouquet and the florist confirms it was bought by Wayne Stern."

"Wait! Were the balloons in a very expensive vase with all the fixings?" Jess got excited.

"Yes, they were."

"Sara Stern had a similar vase of balloons. There has to be a connection."

Colfax mocked her. "Balloons are not rare. Many new mothers get balloons."

"Jess, you have managed to procure some good information. Thank you. Now leave it to us. I don't want anything happening to you."

"Yeah, like getting conked on the head and getting kidnapped." Colfax couldn't help herself.

"Ginny, please..."

"No, Tory. It's OK. Obviously, she has problems with our relationship. But both of you have a point. I must stop acting like I work for the police department."

Jess was not ready to give up. The elaborate balloon bouquet had to be the key. There is no way that two women at the same hospital received the same gift on the same day and the same floor.

"Guys," she called out as she pulled out her phone. "This is a picture of the balloons from Sara's room. Did the one in Tamika's home look exactly like this?

"Yes. I must say it did."

"They must have been bought by the same person. And I am willing to bet my business that person is Wayne Stern."

Trent was quiet as he mulled over Jess' idea.

Colfax was not convinced. "OK. Say we buy this theory. How does this help our case?"

"It might be the twin thing, but when I see two things exactly alike, I know they are related."

"The twin thing! You have a twin! Don't tell me it is a girl. That's why Trent is so fixated on you. I knew it was something," mocked Colfax.

"Officer Colfax!" Jess' tone surprised everyone. "I have had enough of you! Trent, here's the deal. I will no longer work with you if she is around. There is only so much I can take."

"Well, since he already has a partner..." Ginny couldn't help herself.

"Let's see how long you last. He will find out the real you soon enough." Jess practically ran out of the room, slamming the door behind her.

"What did she mean, the real me?"

"She just doesn't realize I have already figured you out."

****

Back in the car, Trent was livid. "Why can't you just leave her alone."

"Trent, she just can't go around acting like she is a detective. You need to do something about her."

"To be a woman, you are so clueless about them. She is just going to keep on because it bothers you."

They rode in silence for a few minutes. Colfax broke the silence. "You are right about me. I did have an agenda when I came to work with you. I wanted to get under your skin and see what makes you tick. When I found out about Jess, I had hit the jackpot. I guess I'm a little jealous of what the two of you have."

Trent didn't respond. He had already known this information. However, he was not going to give her the satisfaction of letting her off the hook.

"OK. I'll say it. I'm sorry. I will leave the two of you alone. Please say something."

"Colfax, I have no words. Let's just solve this case. What do you think our next move should be?"

****

Tamica Parsons and her brother Thomas Parsons were arguing in the hospital room.

"Why did you tell them you were married to Wayne? What do you think is going to happen when the police find out the truth?"

"Thomas, you worry too much. I just need the insurance money to come through. After that we can go wherever we want. Plus, his wife hardly talks to him anymore. She probably doesn't even know he is dead."

"Well, you don't seem too broken up that your love is dead."

"You don't know anything about me. I just am thinking about my baby. He must be taken care of. I can't fall apart now."

****

Jess opened her front door to her best friend Tami's smiling face. She also had a huge pan of her famous tater tot casserole.

"I didn't know you were coming over. Girl, you always know what I need. Your tater tot casserole is my favorite."

Tami and the casserole were the perfect combination to help Jess take her mind off her troubles.

CHAPTER THIRTEEN

Sara Stern was bothered. The message on the answering machine didn't give her much information on the accident. Only that her husband's brakes were cut and that he was dead. She remembered talking to a girl at the nursery about the message. But the details were foggy.

But for some reason, she didn't feel like calling the police back in a hurry. Oh well. She will deal with it when she gets home. He was never in a rush to help her do anything.

Sara didn't even care if anything happened to her. All that mattered to her now was her beautiful baby girl.

****

Colfax was tired. "The car is not telling us anything. Maybe we need to try something else."

"Suppose we start dissecting phone records. If what Jess said is true, maybe Wayne Stern was having an affair. That would show up in his phone logs."

Colfax wasn't convinced. "That doesn't mean murder happened here. Men and women are unfaithful all the time and they don't kill each other."

Trent just shook his head. "How long have you been a cop. Examining the phone records gives us a place to start. And it may give us motive."

"I know. It's just that I have a hard time believing the story about another wife.

"We found Tamica Parsons' information on his emergency contact card in his wallet. A simple DNA test will prove the baby is Wayne Stern's. And when it does, case closed. No motive there."

"We will see, Ginny. But we are going to start with these phone records."

****

The phone records were rather normal. They didn't show anything outstanding. Stern's job called him a lot more frequently in the last month or so. But that was to be expected because his wife was in the last months of pregnancy.

Trent and Colfax decided to visit Stern's place of employment to ask them a few questions about him.

Wayne Stern worked for Adventure Marketing, a marketing firm located in North Atlanta. When the two of them drove up, a valet ran up to park their car.

"We will park ourselves. We are here on police business."

"But sir. It's required that we park all the cars. It's the rule," the valet protested.

Colfax could tell that Trent was about to lose it. "How about this. We will park our own car, but you will still get your tip." She flashed her winning smile.

It worked. The valet showed them where to park. "I will be here when you get back."

****

Trent thought the marketing office was unlike any office he had seen before. There were no cubicles. Instead, there were several short tables with brightly colored chairs. Each table looked like it could only seat 2 people. Some individuals were sitting in chairs alone, talking into headsets. Large, interactive boards filled almost every wall. The chatter of marketers was constant.

"Well, I can't really see Stern working here. These all look like Millennials. Where does a balding, middle-aged man fit in this scenario?" Colfax scanned the room.

"Let's find out. We need to find out who is in charge."

A young man dressed in tight jeans and frilly sleeves on his shirt came up to them. His outfit was topped off with flip flops which showed his poorly manicured toes. "That would be me. Call me Larry. They told me that you are interested in Wayne Stern. Heard the news. It's a shame. Wife just had a baby. Poor guy."

"So, what did Stern do around here? It doesn't seem like this would be his kind of office."

"Well, when the new CEO took over, she changed the entire face of the company. Many old-timers didn't like the changes and they left. Not Wayne. He stayed.

"The powers that be decided to put him in charge of the older accounts. We take care of the new accounts. The system worked."

"Where is Stern's desk? We would like to look through his things." Trent was ready to get to work so they could leave. This was not his kind of place.

"Umm, Wayne didn't have a desk. He was an outside salesman. He worked out of his car. He came in maybe once a month to check in."

"We noticed that he received a lot more calls from work during the last month or so. What was that about?"

"Well, we found out that he wasn't making his visits to our customers in the field. We would call him to ask him what was going on. He would say his wife was having complications with the pregnancy and that he would get back to work right away. He always did."

Trent turned around and walked away.

"Thank you, Larry. We appreciate all the information you have given us."

Outside, Colfax scolded Trent. "You really need to work on your people skills. You were rude to that young man."

"Did you see any work material in the victim's car?"

"No, but he could have taken it out. Maybe it's at his home."

"Then that's our next stop. Oh, and don't forget to tip the valet."

CHAPTER FOURTEEN

"Thomas, go to the car and get the car seat. I am getting discharged in a few. I am ready to go home."

"OK, OK. I'm on my way. Don't rush me."

Tamica was excited to go home. She wanted to begin working on the insurance paperwork. She already had the baby room set up so that would not be a concern.

She thought it clever to name her son Wayne Stern Jr. That would really throw the police off her scent.

"Car seat is here. Now do you know how this thing works? It has too many straps."

****

Jess couldn't eat another bite. Tami's tater tot casserole was the best she had ever had. That could be the pregnancy hormones, but who cares?

She was lounging on her couch thinking about the case. She knew she should just let it go, but she couldn't.

Sara Stern stayed on her mind. Sara had to be Wayne Stern's wife. Why would she make that up?

Well, whatever the case, she would deal with it tomorrow. She was exhausted. She drifted off to sleep on the sofa.

****

Trent and Colfax pulled up to the address on Stern's emergency contact card. It was a cute little house with a small yard. The driveway already had a sportscar and an SUV parked in it, so they parked on the street.

When they rang the bell, Thomas Parsons answered. "Hello officers," he said in a slightly elevated tone. "You came just in time. We just arrived home from the hospital. I am on my way out. Do you need anything from me?"

"Not right now. If we need you, we will contact you."

"My sister is inside resting with the baby. Would you like me to get her?"

"Yes, please." Colfax was trying to be nice even though she really wanted to be sarcastic with him.

Tamica came to into the living room with a robe on. "Thomas, let the police in. Why are you being so rude?"

86

"Tamica…they just…I was going to…"

"Aren't you leaving? I will call you if I need anything.

After Thomas left, Tamica turned on the charm. "Officers please sit down. Can I get you anything?"

This time Trent spoke. "No ma'am. We know you just got home for the hospital. We just wanted to look through some of Mr. Stern's items and see if we can find a clue of some sort. We don't have a warrant. We were hoping to impose on your kindness. May we?"

Tamica pondered. "Ok. Don't wake up Wayne Jr. I just got him to sleep. Feel free to look around."

Trent and Colfax began a systematic search through the house. Colfax searched the bedrooms and kitchen, while Trent examined the living room, bathrooms and garage. It took no time at all.

Colfax thanked Tamica for her time and the two of them left to compare notes.

"Alright Colfax, what did you find?"

"Well, everything seemed normal. I saw pictures of Tamica and her husband. Suits and shoes in the closet. Some shirts embroidered with Adventure Marketing's logo. Normal his and hers stuff."

"Same here. Nothing too much out of the ordinary. However, there were a lot of car fluids in the driveway. I took a sample and will have them examined."

"You are thinking that maybe his breaks were cut here, because if he parked his car in the driveway, anyone could easily have access."

"I am trying to figure out if there was enough fluid in the brakes to drive from here to the hospital to the convention center."

"That is a good question and a hard one to answer. But none of this gives us motive yet."

"We just have to keep looking." Trent started the car and drove off.

CHAPTER FIFTEEN

The lab reports came back that the fluids in the driveway at Tamica Parsons house were oil and transmission fluid. No brake fluid was present.

Trent was not happy. Colfax tried to comfort him. "It seemed that you can't get a break in the case, no pun intended."

"Ginny, none of this makes sense. Why don't we have a motive. And if there is one, why can't we find it? Where were his brakes cut?"

"Well, Tory," she seductively played around with his name, "why don't we retrace his steps from that day."

"That's a good idea. That is something we should have done already. Let's go." Trent was halfway out of the door when he turned around and said, "Don't play those games with me, Colfax. I don't have time."

****

Jess was not happy. Her present mood could not be blamed on hormones. She didn't appreciate Trent and Colfax brushing her off. She was convinced that if Colfax was not there, Trent would have at least listened, even if he didn't agree. But, no. He would not even check to see if her story had any truth to it.

She would have to find a way to reach him. She needed him to pay attention to her for more than one reason. She wanted him to take her seriously. She also wanted his help as she tried to handle her pregnancy.

****

Since Sara Stern had complications with her recovery, she had not been released from the hospital. Baby Wynter Stern was still in NICU. This made it easy for Jess to visit them.

"Hi Mrs. Stern. Do you remember me?"

"Yes, you are the interpreter. Why are you here?"

"I came to check on you and to ask you a few questions."

"OK. That's fine. Have a seat."

"How are you and Wynter doing?"

"Wynter is getting stronger and I am feeling a lot better. Thank you."

"I don't think those are the questions you really want to ask me. You want to know about my husband."

"Yes ma'am, I do. I am an amateur sleuth."

"What do you want to know."

****

Mrs. Stern strongly denied that she was aware of anyone else romantically involved with her husband. Almost too strongly. She said that the name Parsons sounded familiar, but she thought it was someone he worked with. Jess would certainly check out his coworkers and his client list.

This road may be a dead end, but she was still going to explore every avenue. She needed to find a motive.

"You are not a police officer." Jess had to remind herself.

That doesn't matter, she convinced herself. After the blowup with Trent and Colfax, she wasn't about to let them know what she was doing.

****

"I can't believe you roped me into this. Do you know how dangerous this is?"

"And yet, here you are. Good thing you can't say no to me. We won't be long."

Tami drove to the alley where Jess was attacked. It was almost 9:45 pm, around the same time Jess was walking there a few months prior.

"I still don't like it. That's why I have my husband on the phone with us. If anything goes down, he's ready to call the police."

"Thanks a lot. You are such a swell guy."

"Yeah, yeah. I am still confused as to why you won't call your police officer friend," said the voice on the other end of the phone.

"I have my reasons."

Jess rolled down her window. "Here is the alley. Don't pull in. I don't want us to get blocked in."

"So," began Tami, "are you remembering anything?"

"I need to get out."

"Jess, no." But it was too late. She was out of the car, approaching a dumpster.

"I remember this. It smelled like someone had just puked in it. I remember thinking that I was going to add my own vomit to it.

Jess move to the other side of the alley, closer to the building that housed a dry cleaner. "I was over here when I was grabbed from behind. Wait, I was hit on my shoulder. I think the guy aimed for my head, but I moved when I sensed someone behind me.

"Tami, I am remembering! This is where I was lying on the ground as they …"

"Jess are you OK? Let's go."

"Wait Tami. One of the guys has been here recently. I smell him."

"Uh oh. There goes the sniffer again. Honey, that will never hold up in court."

"I'm serious. It's etched in my brain."

Jess slowly came back to the car. Tami let her husband know they were fine as they pulled around the corner.

"Tami! When I was going unconscious one of the times, I heard someone say, "I wonder how the O.C.s will feel about this?"

"OK. We already know it was them, right? Oh…I see. If it was the O.C.s, they wouldn't have asked that question. You have to tell Tory all of this."

"Nope. He and his dragon woman would only scold me for acting like an amateur police officer."

"Well Jess, you are acting like ..."

"Whose side are you on anyway?"

"Yours obviously. I'm here, aren't I?"

****

Jess was walking down a dark alley. The one light in the alley was flickering on an off. A dog barked in the distance. Why did her GPS send her this way? What was she thinking?

"Heeey baby! You shouldn't be walking out here alone. Where is your escort? Why don't you come over here and keep me company?"

Jess began to walk faster to the point of running. At one point she even lost her shoe. The voices in the dark multiplied. She turned to look behind her and ran directly into a wall, or what she thought was a wall. It was a man's chest. She bounced off his chest and fell to the ground. The men descended upon her like vultures. Before she was knocked unconscious, she heard someone say, "Let's initiate the cop first. Go get him."

Jess woke up in tears. She was sweating so bad that her clothes were sticking to her. She got up and ran to her mother's room, sobbing. She curled up in the bed next to her mother.

"Jess, what's wrong? Is it the baby?"

"No, I had a horrible nightmare. It was about the night I was attacked. I remembered something."

Jess paused while she continued to cry. It was like there was a waterfall within her that could not be stopped.

Louisa's heart was in turmoil as she held her daughter and let her cry. She wasn't sure of all that happened that night, but she knew it was awful.

"You need to call the Lieutenant right away."

"No, Mom. I can't. Besides, it's the middle of the night."

"He will come."

Thirty minutes later, Trent was knocking on the door at the Turner home. Louisa let him in and led him to the living room where Jess was sitting on the sofa with her knees drawn up to her chest.

"Lt., I made some banana nut muffins yesterday. I can bring you some with some coffee."

"That would be lovely, Ms. Turner. I would like that."

Trent sat in the armchair across from Jess. He could tell she was in distress. Besides, they hadn't spoken since their blowup.

"Jess. Talk to me."

"While I was having a horrible nightmare, I remembered something about the night I was attacked."

"Take your time."

"I heard one of the guys say something about letting the cop rape me first.

"Also, please don't be mad. I went to the alley where everything happened, and I remembered something else. One of the guys said something like "I wonder what the O.C.s will say about this.""

Louisa came in and silently placed the muffins and coffee on the table. She quickly left the room.

Trent got up and started pacing. This always helped him think. But right now, it was a way to calm his anger.

"Jess, I never told you this. You may have wondered why a homicide lieutenant was handling your case. Well, we had a couple of similar case before yours. However, those young ladies were killed. Your case was the latest one and you were left alive.

"I'm not trying to scare you, but I thought you should know the truth since you believe you should do your own poking around." He couldn't help but to add that at the end.

"What you have just told me confirms a suspicion I had. I haven't told anyone because without Detective Richardson around, I don't know who to trust. I'm going to need you to keep this quiet until I can find out who is working both sides."

"I understand. But does this mean they might attack me again? Am I or my mother in danger? Tory, what am I supposed to do?"

"Keep calm and follow my advice. And stop doing your own investigating. I am going to look after you and your family personally."

"I am sorry that I woke you. I know it's the middle of the night and you have to work later this morning."

"Let that be the least of your worries. You can call me anytime, and I mean that. Do you want me to stay?"

"No, that's OK. I am going to try to go back to sleep. I can't thank you enough for coming."

As Trent walked to his car, he was contemplating his next step. He decided to make it top priority to keep Jess safe.

* *

Trent threw Jess' file on his desk. Things were not adding up. He just wasn't sure what things. He had investigated every shred of evidence there was in the file, but there was not even one person to name as a suspect. The O.C.s graffiti was on the wall at the scene, but that was not enough evidence to say they were behind these heinous crimes.

How were the girls targeted? All of them were attacked in or dragged to an alley. All were walking alone at night. Jess was the only one who received a phone call telling her to report somewhere.

"Hey guys," he yelled out of his office. "Who's the guy who works the gang unit and is familiar with the O.C.s?"

Someone answered. "It's either Watson or Holmes. I can't remember which one."

"Thanks for nothing wise guy."

"Boss, you know I try word association to remember things, so. . ."

"It's Watson. He's a close, personal, friend." Colfax slid into his office and leaned on the wall. What's going on? We got a lead?"

"No. Not yet. Reviewing old cases."

Colfax glanced at his desk and saw Jess' name on the file. She decided it would be in her best interest to stay quiet.

Trent noticed the glance and waited for the fireworks. None came.

Ginny, do you think you can set up a meet with Watson? I have a couple of questions I need to ask him."

"Sure thing, boss."

****

"There is something going on. The LT is looking at us again. He is contacting Watson."

"I am going to handle this right away. You go back to work and remember to remain calm."

****

Trent came back from lunch to find two O.C.s standing outside his door. This had to mean Samuel Guthrie was inside.

"Gentlemen," Trent nodded as he stepped inside. The guards did not respond.

Samuel Guthrie was dressed in a suit that made Trent look like he shopped at a homeless shelter. His tie alone had to cost a couple hundred or more. Not to mention his shoes.

"Well, Guthrie, to what do I owe this honor?"

"We need to talk, Trent. I am not saying that we are saints, but there is some stuff being done that has nothing to do with us. I want to clear our name."

Trent struggled to stop himself from laughing when he realized that Guthrie was serious.

"What exactly would you like to clear up?"

"These rapes and murders. That's not us. We respect our women."

"You respect your women...hmmm."

"I am not saying we haven't done some bad stuff. But these latest things, we didn't do it."

"Your tag was at the scene of all the murders."

"We tag a lot of places. That doesn't mean anything."

"So why are you telling me this."

"Because you need to go out there and find out who really did this instead of looking at us. Stop wasting your time investigating us again," Guthrie smiled. "You need to spend your time protecting your pretty little friend."

Trent didn't even bother to acknowledge his statement. "Who do you think is responsible for this?"

"That's your job to find out. But I will tell you this. When we find out, we will take care of them. No one disgraces us."

"Guthrie, let the police handle it."

His warning went unheeded. Guthrie and his men were already gone.

As the three thugs left, Trent began to consider what was said. Guthrie mentioned 'investigating us again.' He had only reopened the topic of the O.C.s today. Samuel also knew about his relationship with Jess. That information was not common knowledge on the street.

Like it or not, Trent had to finally accept that there was a mole in the department.

CHAPTER SIXTEEN

Jess decided to throw herself into her work. She didn't want to stay at home another day and worry about the things that Trent said.

She took an assignment at a dentist's office. As she and the client were in the waiting room, the TV was on the news, thankfully with the closed caption on. Wayne Stern's death was the topic for the moment. The deaf gentleman was intrigued by the story.

"Did you know the man who was killed had a deaf wife? I know her. They just had a baby girl."

"Wow. That's really sad."

*"I wonder **why** someone killed him."*

That statement made Jess' heart jump. Maybe they had been going about this case the wrong way. Once the motive was known, then it would be easier to figure out who did it.

As soon as her assignment was completed, Jess picked up the phone to call Trent, but paused. She wasn't sure how their working relationship was now. She would have to explore on her own, safely.

She went to the library and began to look up Wayne Stern's history. Both of his parents died several years ago, and he did not have any brothers and sisters. He and Sara Stern were married five years earlier. The birth of their daughter was not yet recorded.

He had been working at his marketing firm for eleven years. On the surface, Stern looked on the up and up.

Wait! There was no record of Wayne and Tamica being married. There was no divorce from Sara mentioned. True, his records might not have been updated. This was something that needed to be checked out.

Once again, she reached for her phone and stopped. She would have to do this on her own.

****

Jess had a hunch. She decided to visit the marketing firm that Wayne Stern worked for.

"Hi," she told the receptionist. . . if you would call her that. She was sitting in an armchair with a headset on. She had on jeans, cute sandals and a tank top.

"I am here to see Wayne Stern."

"Oh my. Sorry to tell you that he is no longer with us."

"He got fired??? Who is handling his accounts? Better yet, who is handling MY account?"

"He had a fatal accident, Ms... I didn't get your name."

"OH! I'm so sorry to hear of his death. I'm Ms. Turner, with Hear Our Hands Sign Language Interpreting Agency."

"Right, right. Well his death was so sudden that we have not yet been able to divide up his accounts."

"I can't believe this. What am I supposed to do? Wait, what about Tamica? Tamica Parsons. They worked closely together, right? Maybe she can help me."

"I don't see how. She is in the art department. Besides, she is on maternity leave."

"Of course, she is." Jess rolled her eyes. "It must be weird working at the same company as your wife."

"Umm, Mrs. Stern didn't work here. I'm not sure where you are getting your information, but ..."

"Fine. I will return when Tamica returns. Thank you."

Jess breathed a sigh of relief as she left the building. She was also very excited. This proves that Tamica Parsons was an imposter. Maybe she was involved in Wayne Stern's death.

****

Jess was deep in thought as she walked towards the valet stand. As she waited, she had an idea. Valets see and hear a lot, but no one every asks them anything.

The valet drove her car up to the stand.

"Here you go, Miss."

Jess slipped him a $20 bill. "Thank you."

"No, thank you!"

"You got a minute? I would like your opinion on something."

"Sure. This is not a busy time of day."

"Are you familiar with sign language interpreters?"

"Uh, I think so. Aren't those the people who stand on stage or on TV flapping their hands?"

Jess chuckled to herself but stayed in character. "That's exactly what I mean. People don't see us in schools, doctor's appointments and the DMV. It's like we are invisible. No one really sees me or takes me seriously."

"I meant no disrespect, Miss. I understand how you feel. I park cars, I bring them back. Half the time they don't even speak to me. It's like I am invisible too.

"I know everyone who comes in and out, except visitors. I have most employees' cars ready in the front of the building before they come through the front doors. With that kind of service, you would think they would be friendlier.

"You are the first person to actually talk to me in weeks."

The conversation was going just where Jess wanted it to go. "Wow. That's cruel. Did Wayne Stern ever treat you like that?"

"He was the worst. But," the valet lowered his voice, "his girl would always tip me a little extra for my discretion. I guess it's OK to tell you this now since he is dead and all."

"Is the young lady's name Tamica?"

"Yep, that's her. A candy apple red Mercedes. Haven't seed her in a while. Guess she had her baby."

She flashed him a bright smile. "Well, I'm Jess. I'm glad we could relate to one another. I will definitely speak if I come back through here again."

"Cool. I'm Roy. That would be a welcome change. And thanks again for the tip."

****

The florist was not a place that Jess enjoyed coming to. True, Jess loved getting flowers, but a flower shop was overwhelming to her keen sense of smell. She always became dizzy. Now being pregnant enhanced the issue. However, there was a job to be done. So, she persevered.

"Good morning, how are you?" A very energetic young lady greeted her. "What can I create for you today?"

"Hello. I need answers more than I need flowers. A couple of days ago, a friend of mine received a huge balloon bouquet that was just beautiful. Wait, it might have been two. Anyway, I might be in the market to get the exact bouquet and I need to know how much it costs."

"Hmmm, I'm not sure which one was bought. Let me check our records from a couple of days ago. Oh, here it is. Two balloon bouquets were purchased. I think I could recreate this. What type of vase do you like?"

"Well, what are my choices?"

"I will get some from the back."

As soon as the young lady went through the double rubber doors that led to the back, Jess leaned over the counter and looked at the screen. The name on the invoice was Wayne Stern!! She took out her phone, snapped a picture and ran out of the front door before the clerk could return.

****

I guess I should go and visit Tamica, Jess thought as she drove towards Ms. Parsons' house.

Tamica answered the knock on the first tap.

"Can I help you?"

"Hi, Ms. Parsons, I work with the police and we are trying to tie up some loose ends concerning your husband's untimely death." Jess hoped she was sounding cop-like.

"Sure, come on in. Our little boy is sleeping. It's a shame he will have to grow up without his father."

As they walked into the living room, Jess couldn't help but notice the beautifully extravagant balloon bouquet. They were the same ones as Sara Stern's.

"Wow, those are amazing! Where did you get them?"

"My husband gave them to me before he died. Actually, the same day he died." Tamica managed to squeeze out a tear.

"I am so sorry for your loss. I guess I should have led with that."

"Now, what did you want to know?"

"Do you know any reason why your husband was at GraphiCon? Was he meeting someone or was he an attendee?"

"Like I told you guys before, I have never even heard of GraphiCon, no less why he was there."

"I'm not going to ask if you know anyone who wanted to harm your husband. That has already been asked. But I would like to know some of his friends. Who did he hang out with?"

"Umm, wow. Well, I know a guy that works at the barber shop on Ponce. They watch sports a lot either at the shop or at Gary's house.

"Let me see if I can find his card. Oh yeah, here it is. His name is Gary Prather."

****

Jess dreaded going to the barbershop. She knew it would be full of men in various stages of maturity. She would have felt better about this if Trent were with her, but that wasn't going to happen.

Gary Prather did not like women in his barbershop. They always started trouble. He didn't care who didn't like it. It was his barbershop and he made the rules.

When Jess walked in the shop, everyone stopped talking. All eyes turned towards Gary.

"Miss, the beauty salon is down the block on the right. You can't miss it."

"Hi. Mr. Prather, Gary Prather? I work with the police. I came to get some information from you."

"I don't have time. I am trying to run a business here. Have a nice day."

Jess moved closer and whispered to barber. "Mr. Prather, unless you want me to tell everyone what type of activities are going on here after hours, I suggest you talk to me privately."

Sometimes, Jess even amazed herself when it came to fooling people.

All of clients began to mumble amongst themselves. Gary got mad.

"Young lady, I don't know what you want, but I am losing my cool with you. Follow me."

"He bought it," Jess thought. Maybe she was on to something.

"Listen lady," he started, "I don't know what your end game is, but I know you are not the police. What do you want?"

"I would like to know about Wayne Stern."

"What's to know? He was a client as well as a friend. We spent a lot of time watching sports, when his wife didn't nag."

"Did she nag a lot?"

"Naturally. She would fuss about him watching sports, going out, and the like. But when he bought his new sports car, she really lost it."

"What did she say about his car?"

"Basically, that the car was not a family car. They were expecting a baby. She got really heated about it. She told him that he wasn't man enough to drive that kind of car.

"Most of the time he ignored her. But as far as I know, that is the only he ever stood up to her. He was very proud to tell everyone here that he told her <u>was</u> macho enough to drive. He had gone and put 'MACHO' on his license plate."

"Now, missy, I don't know how you figured out about my after-hours activities. I would appreciate it if you would keep my gambling quiet or I will tell the police that you are impersonating them."

****

These investigations proved to be very productive. More information about Stern was coming to light, especially his relationship with Tamica Parsons. Where to next?

Her phone rang. Louisa was yelling franticly. "Did you forget you have a doctor's appointment today? Where are you? Sophia said you were out of the office, but you were not on an assignment. WHERE ARE YOU??"

"Oh no! Mom, I forgot. I am on my way to pick you up you right now. I have to stop for gas first."

"Why don't you just drive my car. I don't want to be late to see Dr. Johnson."

"I won't be long. I just feel more comfortable driving my car. I have a lot on my mind. Your car is so fancy, I don't want to think about all of the bells and whistles."

"OK. Just hurry up!"

As she drove to pick up her mom, Jess smiled. To her knowledge, this was the first gentleman that her mother had shown an interest in since her father left. But her mom was always traveling with her friends, so she really didn't know.

****

The doctor's office was a lot busier than last time Jess and her mom were there. Women in various stages of pregnancy were seated, crammed in chairs that seemed entirely too small for their bodies. A few babies in car seats were bundled up contentedly. A little boy about 2 years old was playing a game on his mother's tablet with the volume turned all the way up.

Jess took one glance into the waiting room and turned back towards the door. There was no way that she was going to wait in here with all this commotion. Her head was already spinning. She asked the receptionist about this seeming discrepancy.

"Excuse me, I was just wondering how often an expectant mother needs to come for her checkups?"

115

"Well, Mom, its different with every pregnancy."

"I don't believe I should be back so soon."

"That's something you need to discuss with your doctor."

Wait, did she call me Mom? Jess wasn't sure how she felt about that. She had a few months before she had to decide as to what to do with the baby. So, hearing herself being called a mom was unnerving.

"Ms. Turner." The nurse was cheery, and her scrubs were a beautiful shade of lilac. Instantly, Jess calmed down as she walked to the back. She quietly allowed the nurse to weigh her and take her vitals.

Surprisingly, Louisa was quiet as well.

While in the room waiting for the doctor, Louisa finally spoke. "Jess darling. I'm really worried about you. You are having nightmares; you are running around in dark alleys and you have been doing your own investigations. You need to start thinking about you and the baby's health. You need to rest."

"Mom, where are you getting your information from?"

"Are you trying to tell me it's not true?"

116

"That's not what I'm saying."

"Well, what I am saying is that you are doing too much, and you are not the only one involved."

****

"Jess, after looking at your labs, we have decided that you are a high-risk pregnancy."

"What does that mean?!"

"It means that you are going to have to take it easy. I am not putting you on bedrest now. But if I find out that you are working too hard and not getting enough rest, I will make bedrest mandatory."

Jess looked over at Louisa who had an 'I told you so' expression on her face.

117

CHAPTER SEVENTEEN

"I am so over this case. We need to come to a resolution fast. I need to take some time to put my feet up and relax."

"A fine time to be thinking of a vacation, Colfax. There will still be work to do after this case."

"I am only here on a trial basis. It's up to the higher ups to decide if I stay with you or not. Besides, I really don't like being a third wheel."

Trent chose not to respond to Colfax's taunt. Instead, he refocused on his case.

"I know I keep saying this, but I believe there is one clue that will break this case open. We just have to find it."

At that moment, his phone rang.

"Tory, I need to talk to you and Colfax right now. Let's meet at the diner."

"You sure you want both of us? I'm not sure that is a good idea."

"I'm sure. Both of you are working on this case. Both of you need to hear this."

****

The two officers arrived at the diner. Jess was nowhere to be seen.

"I hope Nancy Drew is not wasting our time. We have better things to do."

"She will be here. And will you please be nice?"

"I won't make any promises."

****

Jess had one more trip to make before going to the diner. She drove past the Stern's house very slowly. She took note of the bright red sports car in the carport. The license plate read "MACHO".

"There's no room for a baby's car seat in that," Jess thought. After that, she sped off to meet Trent and Colfax at the diner.

She also thought that a new car would have several bells, whistles, buttons and knobs. A woman in labor would not want to drive a car like that to the hospital.

****

Jess was nervous as she walked in the diner. Tory and Colfax were seated at a table in the corner. They had ordered coffee and some pastries. She noticed a plate was in front of the empty chair for her. She caught the moment when Trent saw her walk in. He immediately smiled, stood up, and pulled out her chair for her.

"You had us worried. Is everything alright? What's going on?"

"What he really means is what took you so long? We have been waiting for 20 minutes."

Jess chose to direct her words to Trent. "I want to start by saying you will be upset with me. I realize the things I have been doing are exactly what you told me not to do. Let's get that out of the way.

"I have been doing research on my own. Wayne Stern's place of employment knows that Tamica was pregnant but made no connection to them being married. However, the valet confirmed they were dating.

Colfax replied, "That doesn't prove anything. Why are you wasting our time?"

"Next, the florist confirmed that he bought two balloon bouquets, which were exactly alike."

"And . . ."

"His friend the barber says that he remembered the "wife". He explained that he had never met her but appeared to be somewhat a nag from Stern's tone.

"He explained that his wife was very jealous of the times when he hung out with the boys."

"Once again, what does any of this mean?"

"The barber also said that just 6 months ago, the wife was angry because he bought a new sports car. She complained that the car was not suitable for a family. I just saw a sports car with the tag "MACHO" on it. It was parked in Sara Stern's garage."

"Maybe she got the car in the divorce."

"I haven't seen any record of a divorce or a second marriage."

"Tory, please take the time to look at all these pieces. You might be upset with me, but don't turn your back on the evidence."

"Jess, let me walk you to your car. Ginny, I will be right back."

On the way to the car, Trent refused to speak. He was upset and did not want to say anything he would later regret.

They reached the car and Jess turned around to face Trent. "As I mentioned before, I know you are angry. I am not going to make any excuses. What's done is done."

The silence that followed was deafening. The weight of all that Jess had done came crashing down on her. She saw a look on Trent's face that she had never seen before – disappointment.

She opened her car door, started her engine and drove off. She waited until she was around the corner to burst into tears.

****

"Are you going to say anything?" Colfax was starting to feel uneasy with the silence.

Her words didn't matter. Trent kept silent.

"OK I get it. You are mad that Jess went out investigating on her own. I never thought I would say this but, she did turn up some interesting evidence. Why don't we go back to the precinct and review all the evidence? I'm ready to close this case."

She was met with silence once again. Upon arrival at the precinct, Trent went into his office and slammed the door. Moments later, the sounds of crashing and banging came from his office.

The bullpen took cover. Colfax didn't. As she tried to go towards the door, a stapler went through the glass window of the door, narrowly missing her face.

She cried out, from a distance, "Trent!!!! Stop sulking. That will not get us anywhere. Talk to me."

The destruction in the room came to a halt. The other officers were surprised that she was able to tame the beast.

Colfax gingerly stepped into the office. She pretended not to see the chaos everywhere.

"We can start to put all the information we have together and complete the puzzle. Where do you want to start?"

"What was she thinking? I can't protect her if she is going to continue to put herself in harm's way!

"But you are right, Ginny. I need to focus. Let's start with the car."

"We checked the car that crashed at GraphiCon. We need to check out the cars of the suspects."

"Who are we saying are the suspects?" Ginny was getting very excited.

"Sara Stern, Tamica Parsons and Thomas Parsons."

"Perfect. We need to go to the home of all three of them and check out their vehicles. What are we looking for?"

"Not sure. We will know when we see it."

****

After further investigation, Tamica Parsons car was registered to her while the sports car belonging to Sara Stern was registered to Wayne Stern.

"It is not uncommon for married couples to put cars in the name of one spouse." Trent realized this information was not helping them.

"However, Tamica and Wayne Stern had the exact same sports car, just different colors."

"Once again, Ginny, this information is not helping us at all."

"Maybe we should send your girl back out to do more investigating."

"That's it!"

Colfax was confused. "Did I say something right?"

"We can go back to the individuals Jess interviewed, if necessary, and get more information. I'm sure each person she interviewed knew she wasn't a cop. That mean they had no reason to tell her everything."

"I follow you. If we show up with a warrant or the ability to get one, they might be open to talk to us. What about those paternity tests? Did the results ever come in?"

Trent snapped his fingers. "You know, I forgot about those. They really didn't seem relevant. I will find that now."

****

The paternity test results proved that Wayne Stern was the father of both babies.

"Now, that's interesting. How did he manage that?" Colfax was intrigued.

"He was with both women at the same time. We need to decide now if he is a bigamous or had a wife and a mistress.

"If the latter is the case, how do we find out which one is the real wife, and which one is the mistress?" Trent was disgusted.

Colfax blatantly asked, "What does it matter? We are trying to solve a murder, not dole out child support."

****

The re-interviews of the previous witnesses proved to be very productive. Gary Prather, the barber, mentioned that whenever his wife called, it was a video call. Stern said it was because she wanted to see where he was. He talked very loud to her because the shop could hear him even though he was in the restroom.

The florist was very helpful. He was the guy who was on duty when Wayne Stern made his purchase. "He definitely wasn't driving a sports car. He was driving a sedan."

The valet at Stern's place of employment said that after purchasing the new car, he never drove anything other than his prized possession. Even before that, he never drove his wife's car. "And I should know."

Things were starting to shape up.

CHAPTER EIGHTEEN

Thomas Parsons was on edge. He was in a bad situation and had no clue as what to do to fix it. On the last phone call, his life and the life of his family were threatened.

As he finished warming up his frozen dinner in the microwave, he heard a thud at the front door.

"Hmmm. I wasn't expecting anyone." As he looked out of the peephole, he didn't see anyone. He opened the door. Still no one there. As he turned to close the door, he noticed a plastic bag on the porch.

Upon picking up the bag, he realized that it was a severed finger. The blood was oozing out of it while in the bag.

127

Thomas threw down the finger and slammed the door. He figured that it was time to go to the police.

****

"I think I know who did it!" Trent could help but smile. His dimples were deep.

Then his phone rang.

"Guess who that was." As Trent hung up the phone, he was perplexed.

"I don't know. Jess Turner?"

"Colfax. Focus. This is case related."

"One of the wives?"

"Nope, but close."

"The brother?"

"Yes ma'am. He wants to meet with us. Strange, we haven't even been leaning on him that much. But I was going to call all three of them to come in."

"We still can."

****

"Why am I here? I have things to do. I have to nurse my son in about an hour and a half." Tamica Parsons was livid.

"According to the Americans with Disabilities Act, I need an interpreter if you are going to talk to me. It's the law."

"Why are they here? I called and said that I wanted to talk." Thomas was not happy.

Colfax directed all three to the conference room without saying a word. She closed the door behind her as she left.

"That's a fun bunch in there. You ready for this?" Even as Colfax asked, she know he was.

"You know I am ready. We need to wrap this case up."

Colfax asked with concern, "Do we have an interpreter for Mrs. Stern? She is demanding one."

"Got it covered. If there's one thing I have learned from Jess, it's when to hire an interpreter."

"So is Jess on her way?" Colfax slyly asked.

"Nope. That would be a conflict of interest. She is way too involved with this case. A couple of sign language interpreter from her company are on their way."

"Great. When they get here, we need to get this over with."

****

"You really can't hear me?" Tamica mocked. "When Wayne talked about talking to his deaf wife, I always thought he was using a metaphor. No wonder he wasn't happy."

"Tamica! That's enough! Some deaf people can hear a little. Just shut up!"

Sara was too angry to respond.

****

While waiting for the interpreters to arrive, Trent decided to see what Thomas Parsons wanted. He called Parsons out of the conference room.

"Officers, when I was home earlier tonight, someone threw a severed finger on my porch."

"Any why would someone do that?"

"I owe people a lot of money. I have a gambling problem. Now I am in over my head. I need help. I need protection for me and my family."

"Let us examine the finger. We need to get the full story from you while you wait."

"Wait? For what?"

"For the others to arrive. We are closing the case tonight."

****

Trent, Colfax and the interpreters entered the interrogation room. The three suspects were spread out around the rectangular table. Colfax made them crowed around one side of the table.

Tamica was the first to speak. "I have already told you guys that I need to get home to feed my son. Why am I here?"

"We have gathered you all here to finally piece together who killed Wayne Stern."

"Please fill me in. I can't collect on his life insurance policy until all of this gets wrapped up. Besides, why do I have to been here? You could have just called me on the videophone?

Trent decided to allow Colfax to take the lead. He watched the suspects' faces. "We are going to get started. We admit that there were missing pieces, but everything is coming together."

"Thomas Parsons. Your issue earlier this evening cleared up several questions we had remaining."

131

"I don't know how." Parsons voice was shaky. "All I know is that the people I owe money to tossed a cut off finger on my porch. They also threatened my family. How does that help this case?"

"How far would you go to settle that debt?" Trent finally spoke up.

"What do you mean? I tried getting a night job, tried borrowing money from my friends and my sister. I pulled out all the money from my 401K. It just wasn't enough."

"So, when you had an opportunity to make enough to pay off your debt, no matter who you hurt, you jumped at it."

Thomas sighed. "I have been carrying this around long enough. Yes, I am supposed to be paid for cutting Wayne Stern's brakes."

"You idiot!" Tamica hissed at her brother. "Keep your mouth shut until we get a lawyer."

"No, Tamica. I'm tired and I'm scared. My life is out of control and I need to confess. Whatever happens, happens."

Colfax continued. "The next piece we had to put together was who put you up to murdering Wayne Stern."

"We knew who it was. We just didn't have any proof. We had plenty of circumstantial evidence. But that's all it was, circumstantial."

"Until now." Trent's voice broke the silence. "Tamica, you lie about just about everything. You lied about being married to Wayne Stern. You were having an affair and you were having his baby. The affair was a secret, so the three of you had never met face to face. Except Tamica and Thomas, of course."

"Tamica, you didn't even know that Mrs. Stern was really hard-of-hearing and needed and interpreter."

Colfax picked up where he left off. "So, Tamica, being that your brother needed cash because of his gambling problem, killing Wayne Stern would have solved his problems and left you sitting pretty."

"How exactly?"

"Oh, we found out that you have an insurance policy out on him. The payout would keep you comfy for a long time."

"But why would I have him killed? We had a great arrangement. I never wanted him to marry me. I was just excited for the thrill I got fooling around with him. Then I got pregnant. That's when I took out the policy on him. I didn't kill him."

133

"Don't worry, Ms. Parsons. We know. Sara Stern is the one who commissioned your brother to kill her husband."

****

Colfax began the summation. "Sara found out about the affair and the baby. She did her research and discovered Thomas' gambling debts. After that, it was easy to convince him to assist her in the plot to kill her husband."

"You have no proof of any of this. It's just a story that you made up. You invented this entire charade!"

Sara's face was getting red and she was starting to sweat. She was yelling and signing at the same time.

Tamica was baffled. "How did she know about Thomas? Even if she found my number in Wayne's phone, which was not programmed by the way, how would she connect me to Thomas?"

He filled in the blanks. "One day Sara call my sister's phone using a service of some kind. I didn't usually answer her phone, but I thought it was my loan shark looking for me since the number was strange. I was surprised to find out it was Stern's wife.

134

"You're an idiot!" Tamica's disdain for her brother was evident.

"The next time she called me. She started discussing business with me. I asked her if she was worried that the phone service she was using would report her."

"Shut up, Thomas! He's lying!"

"She said she wasn't worried because the interpreters were governed by the FCC and are not allowed to disclose anything they see or hear while on those calls."

Colfax continued as if nothing was said. "The next red flag was the situation with the cars. Since for most of the case we didn't know who the wife was, the sports cars where a real pain. Whenever we interviewed someone, they would talk about a wife and a sportscar. Yet, both of you had one."

"It was then that we had an epiphany. Tamica Parsons car was an automatic transmission. Wayne Stern's car was a manual transmission. Why would a woman in labor chose cram herself into a stick shift sports car instead of her automatic sedan?"

Trent took over from here. "Thomas cut the brakes on the wrong car."

"That just proves that someone was trying to kill me. I would have been the one in the car. My life is in danger. My baby and I could have been killed!"

"Mrs. Stern. That would be believable if you didn't know the breaks were cut. According to the people we interview, your husband never went anywhere without his car. He would never have let you drive his car, especially after your water broke.

"The nurse who helped you out of the car said that the baby's car seat was in the front seat, because it wouldn't fit in the back. They were concerned that you were going to drive home that way. They were going to talk to your husband about it when he arrived at the hospital." Colfax was starting to get irritated as she related these events out loud.

"I was smart enough to have my brother drive us home. He had an SUV. Plus, I bet you didn't know that I, his mistress, was in labor and having my baby at the same hospital. I didn't know he was going to give us the same gift though."

"Shut up!! It's bad enough you were sleeping with my husband. But you had your baby at the same time, at the same hospital! I went to the nursery to check on

136

my baby and I see one with your name. I could have strangled you!"

"There will not be anymore violence." Trent was adamant.

"Well, I still don't think you can prove anything with a car seat in the front of a sports car."

Trent took this one. "We have plenty of evidence that paints a pretty picture of the events that led up to your husband's death. We also have one last thing, or should I say person."

"Yeah Sara. I will testify to all of this."

"I want a lawyer!"

Trent stood up. "I think it's a good idea to get one. I will take you to the room with the videophone."

****

As Thomas Parsons and Sara Stern were led out of the room, they were handcuffed. Thomas was handcuffed in the back, while Sara was in the front. This allowed her to still communicate with her lawyer.

Tamica, for the first time, looked defeated. "I had no idea Thomas and Sara were planning this. If it hadn't been for me and this affair, Wayne would be alive to see his baby boy. Oh yeah, and his baby girl. It's my fault they will never see their father."

Tamica left in tears.

****

"There ae so many unanswered questions. Why was he driving towards GraphiCon? What did he need to do when he got out of the car?"

Trent loved this part. "Well, some things just have a simple explanation. Since the road to the convention center is just a couple of miles from the hospital, he might have been trying to pull over when he realized something was wrong. Most likely, he wasn't an attendee at all.

"Here's the interesting part, remember the mother with the baby stroller he grabbed?"

"Hello. How can anyone forget that?" Colfax didn't see how the question was relevant.

"I don't think he was saying that he had to do something. I think he was telling her that he had <u>two</u> babies."

"That makes total sense. He had just visited the hospital where his children were and his dying thoughts were of his children."

Colfax breathed a sigh of relief. "Good thing this case is solved. I suppose you are going to let Jess know. I mean, she did most of the grunt work."

Trent look troubled. "I'm not sure what I am going to tell her."

✳✳✳✳✳✳✳✳✳✳✳✳✳✳✳✳✳✳✳✳✳✳✳✳✳✳✳✳✳✳

"GraphiCon is in full swing despite the grisly death and murder that occurred there. Nothing has put a damper on *these* festivities. Thousands are expected to flock to the convention center for its final day. If you have not had the opportunity to experience this phenomenon, now is your chance. It's the thrill of a lifetime!"

"Wow, that news reporter seems very excited about GraphiCon. Since the case is closed, why don't you take me to see what it is all about?" Colfax batted her eyelashes, knowing full well she was crossing a line.

"Sure," Trent replied.

Colfax blinked. That was not the answer she expected.

"Are you serious?"

"Yes, I will take you all the way to the train station."

Epilogue

"Did the message say whether it was good or bad news?"

"No, mom. It just said to call the office right away."

"But why? We were just there. And you had a sonogram."

"I'm dialing the number right now. We will soon find out."

The receptionist answered the phone at Dr. Johnson's office and immediately put Jess through to the nurse.

"Hi Jess. Everything's fine. I just wanted to touch bases with you. I know the ultrasound tech did not tell you anything about your sonogram today. They are an outside vendor and they leave all of the explaining to me."

"Oh, OK. I am glad everything is fine. I'm not sure why it was so urgent that I called. You had use worried. "

"Well, there's just one more thing I want to tell you."

"I'm all ears."

"You are having twins!"

****

Trent called Jess to tell her the good news about closing the case. He filled her in on all the details that he could.

"That's wonderful, Tory. Do you have a minute to come over? I need to talk to you."

Trent sighed. "Sure."

****

Trent slowly entered the library at Jess' office. He had a feeling in his gut that he was not going to like what followed.

There were only two chairs in the library. They were plush recliners and they were facing each other. Jess was already seated when he walked in.

"Hi, Tory. Please come in and have a seat." Jess did not look at him as he spoke.

As he sat down, the black hole in Trent's gut grew even bigger. "Just tell me, Jess. Tell me what is going on."

Jess turned her head to look at him and he could see that she had been crying. "There is no easy way to say this, so here it is. I'm pregnant."

The silence in the room was thick. To Jess, it felt like all the air had been sucked out of the room. Finally, Trent spoke.

"I know."

It was Jess' turn to be shocked. "What do you mean, you know?"

"I'm a detective, Jess. I put clues together for a living. You have crazy nightmares. You have been looking pale. You have been acting out of character.

Didn't you know that I would figure it out? I was just waiting to see how long it would be before you told me."

"OK. So why do I have the feeling that you are angry?"

"Well, let's see. I have spent the last few months trying to figure out how to ask you out. The least you could have done is told me you were in a relationship."

"But…"

"No. Let me finish. I really like you and I have a lot of respect for you. But I don't have time for games. So, this is not going to work. I wish you the best."

At that, Trent walked out of the library. Jess didn't move until she heard the outside door slam.

Then she slowly stood up and began to realize that she was going to have to find out who her babies' father was on her own, without Trent's help.

****

As the rain pelted the ground outside, the noise was soothing to Jess. She was seated in her office with the fireplace blazing, even though it wasn't particularly cold outside. In her office, she felt safe. Safe from accusing eyes, safe from Trent and his hurtful words.

She thought of Trent and the tears began to flow, faster and harder than the rain outside. Why couldn't she just have told him the truth? Now it was too late.

"Pull yourself together, Jess." She jumped up from her comfy chair. After she doused the fire and smothered the burning logs, she started locking up her office. She tried to stall, dreading the walk outside in the pouring rain.

She closed the door to the Hear Our Hands office and locked it. She had the feeling that someone was watching her. Jess began to mentally rifle through her purse to see what she could use as a weapon.

At that moment, a man stepped out of the darkness with a huge umbrella.

"Jess," spoke a familiar voice. "How many times have I told you to keep your head on a swivel?"

"Bruce! What are you doing here?!"

"Apparently rescuing a wet damsel. Let's go somewhere we can talk."

"Fine, we can sit in my car."

Long story short, Bruce was Jess' ex-fiancé'. They had an amicable, though extremely painful breakup. The reason for the separation: Bruce wanted children and Jess did not.

In the car, Jess turned on the heat. "Now talk. What are you doing in town and why were you hanging out outside my office?"

"Well, Jess, let me cut to the chase. I heard you were pregnant. I heard how you got pregnant and I want you back."

"What?! Have you lost your mind? Do you. . . How did . . .Forget it."

"Slow down, Jess. One thing at a time."

Jess remained silent, fuming. She wasn't sure who to be mad at.

"My mother told you. Why would she do that?"

Bruce smiled. "Your mother loves me."

"You are capitalizing on my misfortune in order to pursue a relationship with me?"

"You make it sound so bad. Right now, you need friends, friends who really know you. I really know you and I am trying to be here for you. Stop fighting me."

Jess once again continued silent. Too much was happening all at one time.

"I can see that you are trying to figure out what to do. So, let me make this simple."

Bruce got out of the car, opened his umbrella and shut his door. He walked around the car and opened Jess' door. He carefully positioned the umbrella to ensure Jess did not get wet.

He dropped down on one knee. "Jess Turner, will you marry me? You already have the ring."

DOUBLE

BEGINNINGS

COMING SOON

147

www.ingramcontent.com/pod-product-compliance
Lightning Source LLC
Chambersburg PA
CBHW070705280626
47159CB00022B/2145